The Islanders

By Sallie Cochren

All characters and names of characters are fictional and the sole creation of the author. Any resemblance to any person, living or dead, is coincidental.

Sign up for my mailing list to get information on new releases. Go to www.salliecochren.com

No part of this book may be reproduced in any form by mechanical or electronic means including storage and retrieval systems without the author's permission. An exception will be made for reviewers. If leaving a review, you may quote a short excerpt. Your support of the author's rights is appreciated.

ISBN-13: 978-1-7339039-8-1

Copyright Sallie Cochren March 2017

All Rights Reserved

Intro

Gaze upon your crystal
Don't avert your eyes
Be grateful for your leaders
So benevolent and wise
It's time for clear thinking
Time to face your hidden fears
But how will you know
When the danger's really here?

Chapter 1

The waves bore down on her. Above her, all Lakali could see was a dim light that was clouded over by the water that swirled above her head. She could feel a small glimmer of hope as she saw that she was close to the surface. The storm made the waves thrash around her, and it was difficult to pull herself to the surface no matter how hard she pushed with her legs. It was as if the ocean wanted to pull her down into the dark recesses of some hidden abyss. She was almost to the surface when she dared to look down. In that moment, she saw it. It was something made of nightmares!

An enormous cloudy face, watery in substance, as if it was one with the water itself. Its bright green eyes shone in the darkness of the water and beckoned her to come to it. The face swirled with the ocean and stretched upwards, trying to reach her to use its very substance to pull her down and consume her.

Lakali wanted to scream, but she couldn't open her mouth as she was afraid that water would then reach her lungs and she would drown. She looked away. She had to avert her eyes from the monster that waited for her beneath the water. The eyes seemed to almost hypnotize her. If she didn't look away while she still could... No, she didn't dare let herself even think about what would happen.

As she turned away and looked back up to what little light of day was hidden above the water and among the storm clouds, Lakali gave it one last effort. She was exhausted, but she could make it if she pushed herself a little harder. Kicking both feet furiously, she finally approached the surface of the water. She gasped for breath, taking in the sweet oxygen that filled her burning lungs. It felt so good to breathe again, but it didn't last long. The waves crashed around her and tried to push her back under. She fought with every inch of her being to survive and to stay afloat.

When the storm finally cleared, she felt herself treading water easily. But then came the silence, a silence so eerie that Lakali wanted to scream. It was unnatural, and there was something dark and sinister around her. She dared to look down, straining to see what she could under the ripples of water, and she could see a bright neon green glow moving back and forth in the water below her. Then, she felt the pull on her legs. Something was drawing her downward. She kicked and shouted, using all of her strength to try to break free. But whatever had hold of her was too strong, and she couldn't free herself.

Lakali found herself being pulled down into the water. She was going deeper and deeper beneath the surface. The light of day was getting dimmer as she began rapidly plummeting to the ocean below until all she could see above her was water and below her was a blackness that she knew was about to consume her forever.

Lakali was confused. As she sat on the floor of her small hut, she felt unsure about where she was. It took a moment to get her bearings. The room was familiar. There was the antique rocking chair where she passed many hours sitting and reflecting on the island that she called home. She loved her home. The island was about the most beautiful place she could imagine living, not that she could really imagine living anywhere else. The island was the only place she or any of the other islanders had ever lived. Perhaps their ancestors had known other places when they moved here long ago, but once here, they had no desire to leave their island paradise. Their descendants still prospered from their wise decision to remain here. Their families and numbers had grown. Now, there were about twelve hundred people who inhabited the island. It was a peaceful existence, and Lakali mostly reflected on how good her life was. She and her friends had plenty to eat. The island was ripe for growing food. Hunters found plenty of wild birds and small prey to cook. Fishermen collected fish from the ocean daily. No one hungered or went without shelter. It was truly a paradise. Perhaps that was why no one who came here had ever left.

    Fortunately for the islanders, their island wasn't easily spotted by passing ships. It seemed like it was now hidden, satisfied with the many islanders who called it their home. Otherwise, people would surely still be coming to settle here. Then, their island would soon be overflowing with people who would never want to leave. As it was, Lakali couldn't recall anyone new ever coming to the island. She was glad that they were able to enjoy their homeland without being overcrowded and running low on resources.

    Still, Lakali remembered hearing the history of their ancestors and how easily they had found the island so long ago. It was funny, though. She remembered the stories, but she couldn't recall who had told them to her. That wasn't important anyway. What was important was that the island had been found. Their ancestors had known instantly to settle here. It was as if the island had invited them, almost as if it had called to them to come here to settle down and start their new lives. They had no doubts. They had known this was where they were supposed to start over, having fled their homeland when war had broken out.

Lakali wondered why the island didn't still call to passing ships. Was it truly satisfied with the islanders who loved it so much? It filled Lakali with pride to know that the island was happy with those who lived here.

Lakali took a deep breath. She didn't know why, but she felt exhausted. She looked down to see her hands were trembling as they might do if she had awoken from a bad nightmare. But she hadn't been sleeping. She was sitting on the mat on the floor of her hut and was holding the familiar turquoise-rimmed trinket box in her hands. It was her special box. Every adult on the island had one. The boxes were the standard present for any islander when they reached their sixteenth birthday. Lakali had proudly owned hers for five years now. Every afternoon, she sat on the mat in her hut and held the box. It was said that the trinket boxes had special powers to help people think clearly. Perhaps that was why the islanders cherished them so much.

After a few minutes of breathing deeply and clearing her head, Lakali closed the small box and returned it to its safe place on the shelf by her rocking chair. She got up and stretched, once again noticing that her hand was still shaking a bit. She couldn't figure out what had upset her so badly. Like all of the islanders, she lost track of time while she was holding her trinket box. She wasn't sure how much of the day had passed.

Lakali walked outside. It was still light out. Judging by where the sun was in the sky, there were probably two or three more hours until sunset. She looked to the nearest hut which stood about twenty-five feet to the east. Akoni was coming out of his hut. He raised his arms up high and gave a big yawn.

"Did you think clearly?" Lakali shouted.

Akoni looked Lakali's way.

"I think so," he answered.

It was hard to know since the memories of exactly what he had been thinking about had faded. As soon as the box was closed, any trace memories he had quickly left him and all he could recall was what had happened before he had entered his hut. He straightened his posture and smiled. He remembered that quite clearly. He had been flirting with Lakali. She was by far the prettiest girl on the island. She had golden brown skin and long dark hair that hung straight and met her waistline. Her figure was proportioned just right for a girl who was five-feet-eight-inches tall. She stood barely six inches shorter than him. Akoni envisioned himself drawing Lakali close to him and leaning down to kiss her soft lips.

"How about you?" he called to Lakali. "Were you able to clear your head?"

"I think so," Lakali replied, but she didn't sound convincing.

Akoni looked concerned. There was something wrong with his girlfriend.

"Lakali, what is it?" he called. "Are you alright?"

Lakali nodded.

"Of course," she shouted. "I'm fine."

She turned away and walked toward the beach which was about one hundred fifty feet to the north of her hut. Akoni watched her, still concerned as he could tell something wasn't quite right. Lakali walked up to the ocean and kept walking until she felt her ankles submerged by the water coming in with the waves. She stopped and caught her breath.

She didn't know what was wrong, but something didn't feel right. Whatever had caused her trepidation had something to do with the ocean. Why couldn't she remember what had upset her? She closed her eyes, willing the memories to come to her. But none came. The last hour of her life was gone from her thoughts. She had no recollection of anything that had happened.

Lakali was startled when she felt two warm hands come around her waist and pull her backward. She jumped and made a startled noise.

"Sorry. I didn't mean to scare you," Akoni said as he clasped his arms in front of Lakali and held her tightly.

He smelled the coconut fragrance in her hair and took a deep breath. Even her hair smelled heavenly.

Lakali blushed. Maybe she couldn't remember the past hour of her life, but she *could* remember what she had been doing prior to that. She had been flirting with Akoni and had told him how strong and handsome he was. Of course, Lakali wasn't the only one to think so. Akoni was indeed attractive. He had tan skin and dark hair like her. Only, his hair came just a few inches below his shoulders. He kept it pulled back and secured it with a hair tie behind his neck.

Lakali wasn't one of those girls who went around flirting with guys. Even though Akoni was her boyfriend, Lakali was more reserved than some of the girls on the island. She was a bit embarrassed now as she thought about all of the compliments she had given him. She had even winked at him! She had been almost as flirtatious as her friend, Caristiona, had been when she had first met Amzi. It hadn't taken long for Caristiona to get Amzi to marry her. Was that what Lakali had been doing wrong? Had she not been flirting enough with Akoni? If that was the case and if she kept flirting with him like she had that morning, soon Akoni would be dropping down to one knee and he would propose to her!

"A seashell for your thoughts?" Akoni asked.

Lakali laughed.

"What?" Akoni asked curiously.

"My thoughts?" she asked.

"Yes, please tell me what's on your mind," Akoni answered.

"I can't, because I don't know," Lakali replied.

That was partly true. She couldn't remember what had upset her. Whatever had happened in her clear-thinking session would never be revealed to her. Perhaps that was a good thing. Lakali didn't like how today's session had made her feel. It was probably for the best if she forgot all about it. As for her other thoughts, Lakali sure wasn't going to tell Akoni that she had been wondering if she needed to flirt more to get him to marry her!

"You don't know what you're thinking?" Akoni teased.

"I guess that didn't come out right. I was just wondering about the clear-thinking session," Lakali explained. "I was wondering what I had been thinking of then."

Akoni sighed.

"I do wish that we could remember more about our clear-thinking sessions," he said. "It would make things easier. Don't you think so?"

"I don't know," Lakali said nervously.

She wasn't sure what she wanted to remember.

"I think the point is to *not* remember," she said. "Then, our subconscious memories can help us to make wise decisions. I think that our leaders are very smart to give us our clear-thinking sessions."

"I suppose," Akoni replied. "I just couldn't help but notice how upset you looked when you came out from your session."

"I'm fine," Lakali lied. "Nothing bad would come to us in our clear-thinking sessions. The leaders wouldn't allow it."

"Of course not," Akoni agreed. "Perhaps you're just tired."

Lakali leaned her head back so that it was resting on Akoni's shoulder.

"Perhaps I am," she said. "That must be it."

"Then, you should go take a nap," Akoni suggested. "There's no urgent work to be done. Go and rest."

Akoni withdrew his hands enough to allow Lakali to turn around and face him, but he still held his hands on Lakali's waist. Her skin was soft. She was wearing a halter top and shorts, the typical attire for most of the young women on the island. Lakali put her hands on Akoni's bare chest and looked up at him.

"You're always thinking of me," she said. "No one cares more about me."

"They'd better not!" Akoni replied as he pulled her to him.

Lakali let her hands find their way around Akoni's neck and didn't resist him as he pulled her close. She closed her eyes as he leaned his head down and kissed her softly on the lips. After he kissed her, she gently pulled away and sighed.

"You always make me feel better," she said. "Walk me to my hut?"

"Of course," Akoni replied.

When they got to her hut, Akoni stole one more kiss before letting her go. He headed out further down the shore to help the fishermen finish cleaning their catch for the day.

As Akoni left, Lakali watched him. She was lucky to have someone like Akoni in her life. Some girls didn't have such an attentive boyfriend. As comfortable as that thought was and even though she could still taste Akoni's lips on hers, there was still a feeling of discomfort gnawing at her. Lakali let her gaze fall back to the ocean. A cold chill ran through her body. Indeed, whatever was bothering her had to do with the ocean, and she knew that the way she was feeling had been brought on by her clear-thinking session. But it didn't make sense. She always felt so relaxed after the sessions. What had made today's session different?

Lakali wondered if she should go and speak to the leaders, but she knew they were busy. They didn't like the islanders questioning how they ran things. Would they be upset that she was suggesting something had gone wrong in one of the clear-thinking sessions? She decided it was best to wait. Surely, tomorrow's session would clear her mind and whatever went wrong today would be resolved. Perhaps that nap would help. She walked into her hut and went to lie down, intent on forgetting about whatever it was that had upset her.

Chapter 2

Lakali dug her nails in as deeply as she could. She could feel the sand crumbling under her fingers as they dug into the giant boulder that she was hanging onto. She hung tightly to the rock about fifty feet off the ground. The boulder was slanted at about a forty-five-degree angle, and there were very few places to get a good grip on it. The way down was littered with jagged rocks and sharp edges of stones that jutted out from the boulder, waiting to rip into the flesh of anyone unfortunate enough to cross paths with them.

Lakali could feel her feet slipping. She had found a couple of small footholds in her desperation to not fall any further down the cliff than she had already come. Her fingers kept slipping. The loose gravel continued to be a problem, making it impossible for her to get a good grip with her fingers. No matter how hard she tried, she couldn't seem to clutch onto the rock enough to keep herself from falling. Lakali had no idea how she had gotten here. She had simply found herself slipping down the rock and feeling the sharpness of the protruding smaller rocks that had cut into her thigh.

Her leg was burning, and she could feel blood slowly oozing out and running down her left leg. She had no idea how badly she had been hurt. There was no way to get a good look at her leg without losing whatever small grip she had on the rock.

Lakali found herself feeling dizzy, and a gentle blackness tried to overcome her. She felt a swift nausea come over her. For a moment, she thought she was going to throw up. No. Not now!

She had to keep a clear head. She closed her eyes and put her head close to the rock, trying to steady her breathing. She took slow, deep breaths and willed herself to be in another place, anywhere but here.

She tried to picture herself lying on the beach with Akoni, lying with her head on his chest and feeling the warmth of his body next to hers. She thought of how he liked to stroke her hair and kiss her on her forehead as they relaxed in the sun together. For a moment, she thought she could do this. She could hang on and not give up if she just filled her mind with thoughts of Akoni. She could endure anything and survive, knowing that she had his arms to rush back to.

Lakali tried to not think about how dismal her situation was. Worries about how she was ever going to get out of this predicament would do nothing to ensure her survival. She knew that there had to be a way off of this rock and to the safety of the ground below. Slowly, once she felt her breathing had steadied itself, she moved her head away from the rock just a few inches, enough to look down to try to assess how she was going to get down.

It was scary to look below. She didn't see any reasonable way to get down. There were very few places to get a grip on the rock, but she knew she had to try. She couldn't stay up here forever, and she could sense that she was losing a lot of blood from the cut on her leg.

Slowly, Lakali moved her left leg and tried to slide it downward, finding another small groove in the rock where she tried to wedge it. Her heart was beating so quickly that she felt like it was going to explode. She heard the sound of loose gravel falling down as her foot freed it from the rock it had attached itself to. Lakali took a deep breath and let it out slowly. As she exhaled, she slid her left hand downward, finding another groove where she could rest it. That was good. She was one step closer to reaching the bottom and getting to safety.

Taking another deep breath and exhaling, she began to move her right leg downward. But as she felt desperately for a groove where she could place her foot, she found none. She scrambled to find the groove where it had been resting before, but all the movement made what small grip she had on the rock loosen. Her fingers started to fall from their resting place. In a moment of terror, she screamed as she lost her grip on the rock altogether and her body started sliding rapidly down the boulder. She could feel the jagged rocks tearing into her skin as she slid over them. She would have cried out in pain if she could have caught her breath fast enough to do so.

The next thing Lakali knew, she was no longer attached to the rock. She was now freefalling. As she caught sight of the ground below, she saw sharp jagged rocks pointing upwards directly underneath her. She was about to be impaled and watched in horror as she saw the ground approaching, getting closer and closer. She closed her eyes and thought one last time of Akoni, regretting that she would never see him again.

Lakali awoke from her clear-thinking session within seconds of nearly crashing upon the pointed rocks. She opened her eyes and could feel her chest heaving up and down as her breathing was rapid and out of control. She was hyperventilating and knew she needed to calm herself. She had to slow her breathing, but it was hard to do. She felt as if she was falling and could still see those jagged rocks poised, ready to thrust themselves through her torso and kill her instantly.

Lakali had a moment of panic and looked to her leg, expecting to see a deep cut oozing blood. She could see no sign of injury. But to make sure, she straightened her leg out and ran her hands over it, feeling for any cuts. Slowly, she began to realize that it had all been in her head, something brought on by the clear-thinking session. Why was this happening to her? Lakali didn't understand any of it. It felt more like a nightmare than a time to clear her head. Two days in a row that something had gone wrong with the session... She was sure that she was the only islander experiencing this. She didn't know what to do. She wanted to talk to Akoni, but she felt like there was something wrong with her. She didn't want Akoni to think that she was a freak.

It took Lakali several minutes to clear her head and get her breathing and heartrate under control. She didn't want to move. She just wanted to curl up and lie down. Perhaps she was tired, like Akoni had mentioned yesterday. Maybe she wasn't getting enough sleep. What she needed to do was to take another nap. Yet she had napped for two hours after yesterday's session and had slept over eight hours last night. How much sleep could she possibly need? She didn't feel sleepy. In fact, she was wide awake.

Lakali's thoughts were interrupted when she heard a light knock on the door of her hut.

"Lakali?" Akoni called.

Lakali got up and walked slowly to the door. When she got to the door, she looked down and saw that her hand was shaking just like yesterday. She grabbed her right hand with her left one and tried to hold it steady. She took a couple of deep breaths and braced herself to open the door. She didn't want

Akoni to see how upset she was.

"Lakali?" Akoni called again. "Are you alright?"

Taking one last deep breath and exhaling, Lakali opened the door. Akoni's worried face greeted her.

"Of course," she answered. "I'm fine."

"I was concerned," Akoni said. "You always come out right away after a clear-thinking session."

"I was just thinking on some things," Lakali said, as she stepped aside and let Akoni in.

The two of them sat down together on the cot that served as both a bed and a sofa. The huts were small and consisted of one room. The islanders needed a little privacy. The huts afforded them that, but there were very few amenities. The cot was pushed up against the side of the hut. It wasn't the most comfortable place to sit, but it was sufficient. Many islanders chose to sleep in hammocks that were strung up in the corners of their huts. There were also outside hammocks. But during most of the year, the mosquitoes were too busy looking for people to bite for the islanders to want to sleep outside at night.

"Did you not do enough thinking during the session?" Akoni asked. "And you needed to think some more?"

Lakali laughed.

"I guess so," she said.

She still felt shaky, but she was beginning to feel safe now that she was with Akoni. He was so strong and muscular. Surely, he wouldn't let anything bad happen to her.

Akoni reached over and brushed some hair off of Lakali's face and gently pushed it to rest behind her ear.

"I worry about you," he said.

"Why?" she asked. "There's nothing to worry about. I told you that I'm fine."

She wondered if he had seen her hand shaking. Had he picked up on how upset she was? Lakali was determined to be strong and not let him know how scared she really was.

"Hmm," Akoni said. "I hope that's true. I don't know what I would do if I were to ever lose you."

"Lose me?" Lakali asked. "Why would you lose me?"

"I don't know," Akoni answered. "You just seem very distant lately."

Lakali knew she had to get Akoni's mind off of her well-being. She reached her hands up and placed them around Akoni's neck. She pulled him to her and kissed him slowly. He put his arms around her waist and pulled her even closer to him. He pushed her downward onto the cot and leaned over her, kissing her gently. He moved his mouth to her neck and kissed her softly. Then, he returned his mouth to meet hers, and they kissed each other eagerly. Lakali pulled her lips away, but she still held Akoni close. She looked into his eyes.

"I love you," she said.

"I love you, too," Akoni replied.

"Please don't worry about me," Lakali said. "I'm fine. Really."

"I'll always worry about you," Akoni said. "That's a boyfriend's job, isn't it?"

"I suppose," Lakali answered.

Akoni leaned in and kissed Lakali again. He knew he had work that needed to be done, but he couldn't seem to drag himself away from her. It felt so good to be here with her and to feel her soft body next to his. He kissed her again before finally willing himself to stop. He pulled away and sat up.

"What?" Lakali asked, not sure why he had

stopped.

"I've got work to do," he said. "I'd much rather stay here with you. But the last time I got sidetracked like this, the others noticed I wasn't there. Some of the workers were annoyed, saying that I wasn't carrying my share of the workload. If I show up late again today..."

Lakali sighed.

"It's not fair," she complained.

Akoni looked down at his girlfriend. He pulled her up to a sitting position and put his hands around her waist, drawing her to him and kissing her one more time.

"No, it's definitely not fair," he said. "But I'll be thinking about you the whole time I'm there."

"You'd better be," Lakali said.

Akoni got up and regretfully walked to the door. He turned to face Lakali before leaving.

"You know, if those guys had a girlfriend even half as beautiful as you, then I'm sure they'd understand," he said.

Lakali smiled. She watched Akoni leave and pulled her knees up to her chest, clasping her arms around them. She had almost forgotten about the nasty memory. But as soon as Akoni left, it came back to her. She'd much rather remember the taste of Akoni's lips. But instead, all she could see was jagged rocks ready to tear at her flesh. She couldn't shake the memory from her head.

Lakali got up and stretched. She walked outside and took in some fresh air and sunshine. Surely, being out here would clear her head. She looked at the sun in the sky and knew that she too should get to work. She was supposed to go help some of the women who were doing laundry in a nearby stream. She went back into the hut and gathered up a few of her own clothes and started heading toward the stream. She walked among the trees that lined the way. Once she got there, several women had already started to scrub the dirty clothing. Lakali kneeled down beside Bakita. She apologized for being tardy. Bakita was an older woman in her mid-fifties. Bakita smiled.

"No worries," Bakita said. "It's still early. There are enough hours left in the sunlight to finish. Besides, I'm sure a young woman like yourself has other things to occupy her mind."

Lakali smiled. Bakita was a kind woman, and Lakali liked her. They had formed a close friendship. Even though they were twenty-four years apart in age, it didn't matter to Lakali. She enjoyed spending time with Bakita and was glad she had been assigned to Bakita's work group.

"I suppose," Lakali said. "But those things don't count as work."

Bakita laughed loudly.

"Not if you're doing them right," she joked.

Lakali blushed, and Bakita laughed again.

"I didn't mean..." Lakali started to speak.

"Of course not," Bakita answered. "You're a good girl. You just better keep that Akoni in line. We all see the way he looks at you. You make him put a ring on that finger first. You deserve the best devotion he could give you."

"I'll try," Lakali replied.

"Don't try. Do!" Bakita said. "That young man is crazy about you. It's about time that he makes a permanent commitment. It's been too long since we've been able to enjoy a good wedding party! I'll make the cake myself."

Lakali laughed.

"So, what?" Lakali asked. "I'm supposed to tell Akoni that he has to marry me because the islanders are getting anxious for a wedding party and your cake?"

"Whatever works," Bakita answered. "Us women have to do what we can to get these guys to commit to us, don't we?"

"Then, what trick did you use?" Lakali asked.

"Oh, it was simple really," Bakita replied. "I flirted with another man and told Hachuo that if he didn't marry me, this other man was ready to do so. Hachuo became so jealous that he said he would go out and fight that man right away. I told him that I wouldn't be with anyone who had such a temper and that if he wanted to win me, he would need to marry me and then we could both forget all about that other man."

"And it worked?" Lakali asked.

"Like a charm!" Bakita answered. "Have I not been with him ever since?"

"Well, I'd say he was the winner," Lakali said. "It's a good thing he cooperated and stole you away from that other man before you married him instead!"

Bakita laughed.

"What?" Lakali asked.

"It's just funny," Bakita said. "If Hachuo had only known..."

"Known what?" Lakali inquired.

"That other man was in love with someone else," Bakita answered. "He tolerated my flirting because he was too nice to tell me to stop. Besides, I think he knew what I was doing. Everyone knew that I loved Hachuo. Even if that other man had been in love with me instead of someone else, I wouldn't have married him if he would have asked me. I only had eyes for Hachuo!"

"Well then, it's good Hachuo didn't know," Lakali said.

"Yes, it is," Bakita agreed.

They continued chatting and telling stories as they washed their clothes, and Lakali forgot all about the nasty memories from her clear-thinking session. When they were done and the sun was beginning to set, Lakali picked up her basket of clothes and prepared to go back to her hut.

"Now, remember what I said," Bakita called after her. "Don't let Akoni steal too many kisses until he puts a ring on your finger! If you give him too much now, that boy will never make a commitment!"

Lakali nodded.

"Thanks for the advice," she said, and she turned and began the walk home.

About that time, a black cat came along to say hello. He was a friend to the islanders, and his name was Nightfall. Lakali liked cats. He was the only one who she had made friends with. Lakali greeted him and stroked his fur. Nightfall purred and rubbed against her. Then, he went on his way to visit another islander.

That evening, Lakali sat with Akoni and several other islanders around a campfire on the beach as they had a fish fry. The food was delicious. Everyone was enjoying themselves as the islanders sat around laughing and telling stories. Lakali leaned against Akoni, and he held her close.

"This is nice," Lakali whispered. "I wish we could stay like this forever."

Akoni kissed Lakali on the head.

"Me too," he said. "I take it you had a nice day."

"Yes," Lakali answered, keeping her voice low so as to not disturb the other islanders' conversations. "Bakita and I had a nice chat while we were doing the laundry."

"And what things did you talk about? Or

should I say *who* did you talk about?" Akoni whispered. "I'm sure you had all sorts of gossip to chat about."

"If you really want to know, we talked about you," Lakali replied.

Lakali pulled away from Akoni just enough to look at him.

"Oh, really?" Akoni raised his eyebrows. "Should I be worried?"

"Maybe. Maybe not," Lakali answered.

"Now that doesn't seem fair," Akoni whispered back. "You tell someone you were talking about them, but then you won't tell them what you said?"

"You were the one who asked me," Lakali reminded him. "Would you have preferred I lie?"

"Hmm," Akoni answered. "I'm not sure. Can you at least tell me if I should be worried?"

"I think you're good for now," Lakali replied honestly.

Perhaps eventually, she would have to think more about what Bakita had said. Perhaps she would have to work harder to get Akoni to marry her. But for now, she was happy to have him as her boyfriend. She couldn't imagine her life without him, and she certainly had no plans to break up with him.

"For now?" Akoni questioned. "You certainly do like to leave a guy guessing, don't you? What am I going to do with you?"

"I can think of one thing you can do with me," Lakali whispered.

"Yes?" Akoni asked playfully.

"Kiss me," Lakali replied.

"I think that could be arranged," Akoni said and then kissed her.

The kiss didn't last long.

"There are too many people around us," Akoni

23

whispered.

Bakita was looking in their direction. Lakali noticed she was giving her a look of disapproval. Bakita then pointed to the wedding ring on her finger. Lakali returned her smile and then turned back to Akoni.

"That's true," she replied. "We should probably finish our meal."

"That's not a bad idea either," Akoni said. "I'm still hungry. It's been a long day."

"You get too distracted talking to me," Lakali observed. "Eat."

Akoni nodded and dove back into his food. When the meal was over and everything was cleaned up, most of the islanders retired to their huts for the evening. Akoni walked Lakali to her hut. He drew her close to him with his hands on her waist and reached down to give her a soft kiss.

"Invite me in?" he asked. "We could finish what we started at dinner. There's nobody around to see us now."

Lakali reached up and kissed Akoni, taking her sweet time. Reluctantly, she finally pulled away.

"Well?" Akoni asked. "Wouldn't you prefer the privacy of your hut?"

Lakali wanted to invite Akoni in, but she thought that maybe Bakita was right. Maybe she was allowing Akoni too much. She wanted to be happily married to him someday just like Bakita was happily married to Hachuo. Even if Akoni wasn't ready yet, perhaps she shouldn't be so free with her kisses.

"I'm tired," Lakali lied. "I think we should call it a night and see each other tomorrow."

"Oh. Okay," Akoni said, sounding disappointed and surprised.

He kissed Lakali again, letting his lips linger

on hers longer this time. For a moment, Lakali thought of telling him that she had changed her mind, but then she pulled away. She would be strong.

"I'll see you tomorrow," she said.

"Yeah, tomorrow," Akoni replied. "Sweet dreams."

Lakali had a flashback to the nightmare she had had in her clear-thinking session. She felt herself shudder just a little. Akoni noticed it.

"Lakali?" he asked. "What's wrong?"

"Nothing," Lakali lied. "I just got a chill. The breeze is a bit cool."

Akoni wasn't sure that was all that was wrong with his girlfriend, but he wouldn't press her for more information.

"Oh. Then, you should get inside and get to bed," he said. "I hope you're not getting sick."

"No, I'm fine," Lakali replied. "Stop worrying about me so much."

"I'm not sure I can ever do that," Akoni said truthfully. "But I'll let you get to sleep now. I'll see you in the morning."

"Okay," Lakali replied and went into her hut, closing the door behind her.

She went to her cot and laid down, hoping that any dreams she had would be good ones.

Chapter 3

"Do you promise to love and care for Lakali for the rest of your life?" the man asked.

His name was Kalepo. He was the descendent of a man who had captained a ship that had come to the island long ago. Because some ship captains, including Kalepo's ancestor, had the ability to marry people, the islanders made a rule that any of their descendants could do so as well.

"I do," Akoni replied.

"And do you, Lakali, promise to love and care for Akoni for the rest of your life?" Kalepo asked.

"Of course I do," Lakali replied.

"Then, you are now husband and wife," Kalepo announced. "You may kiss the bride!"

Akoni leaned down and kissed Lakali passionately, more passionately than he had ever kissed her before. The kiss seemed to last forever. Neither of them could pull themselves away from each other.

The islanders started to cheer and laugh.

"The ring! The ring!" Bakita shouted happily. "It's time to put the ring on Lakali's finger!"

Akoni pulled away from Lakali.

"Yes, I believe Bakita is right," Kalepo agreed. "It is time for the rings."

There were only so many wedding rings on the island. It was customary when a new couple got married that some of their married friends would give their rings to them.

Bakita had given her ring to Akoni so that he could in turn give it to Lakali. Hachuo had donated his also, and Akoni would now be wearing his ring.

"For my bride," Akoni said and gently placed Lakali's ring on her finger.

She then took his ring from her pocket and placed it on his finger also. Akoni leaned down for another kiss.

"Here they are, the new happy couple!" Kalepo shouted happily.

No one used last names on the island, not anymore. That had gone away a long time ago.

Bakita ran up to Lakali and gave her a big hug.

"You look so beautiful," Bakita said.

Lakali did indeed look radiant. She was wearing a white skirt and had a garland of pink carnations draped around her neck. It hung to her waist so that it covered part of her midriff that the white halter top left exposed. She had white and yellow flowers pinned to her hair.

Akoni was looking handsome also. He was wearing a white t-shirt and a black tie. He also wore denim jeans that had been cut off at the knees. It was about as formal as he would ever get. Not that he needed formal wear. He would look good no matter what he was wearing.

"Everyone, it's time to celebrate!" Kalepo shouted. "Bakita, break out that wedding cake!"

The islanders all went to the beach where a big table had been spread out with all sorts of food - fried fish, boiled potatoes, an abundance of fresh vegetables for salads and Bakita's gloriously-sweetened wedding cake. She had even put some cocoa in it to add to its flavor.

Some of the islanders got out their instruments and started playing for the party. The drums were the primary instruments used, but they had some string instruments that they played as well. The music was lively and energizing. People started dancing and eating. Everyone was having a great time.

"Dance with me!" Akoni said.

Lakali was glad to oblige. They started dancing on the beach, jumping about and throwing their arms around wildly, circling each other. Then, as couples danced all around them, Akoni stopped dancing. He took hold of Lakali and pulled her close to him, leaning down to kiss her. Overhead, the sky started to darken. A storm was coming in.

"Akoni, the weather..." Lakali found herself becoming distracted.

The music became distant. Thunder sounded in the background. Akoni didn't seem to mind.

"Come with me!" he said. "Let's go play in the ocean!"

Lakali was afraid. It was as if she had just had the nightmare. Even though she hadn't remembered it earlier, she could now sense some of the things she had seen in her previous dream, if that's what she could call it. It had been during a clear-thinking session, and she hadn't been asleep. Still, it was as much like a dream as any she had ever had while sleeping. Lakali now remembered the pull of the water and the feeling that something was waiting for her beneath the waves.

"Akoni, no," she said. "I don't want to."

"Trust me," Akoni replied and started dragging her against her will to the water.

"No, Akoni!" Lakali protested.

But Akoni wouldn't listen. He had a tight grip on her arm and was pulling her into the water now. Lakali looked to the beach behind them. It was empty. There was no one around. The wedding feast was gone, even the table. There was no sign of any islander anywhere. Lakali glanced down to her hand. There was no wedding ring.

"Where is it?!" she started screaming.

"Where's what?" Akoni asked. "You're not making any sense. Come on, Lakali. Come with me. We'll play in the ocean!"

"But I don't want to," Lakali said. "It isn't safe."

She tried to resist him, but he kept tugging on her. Soon, they were waist-high in the water.

"Just a little further," Akoni insisted and again brought her further into the ocean against her will.

Soon, Lakali was so deep in the waves that she had to tread water to stay afloat. She suddenly had the stark realization that she was all alone. Where was Akoni? Had he been dragged under the water, or had he never been there at all? Lakali started screaming.

"Akoni! Akoni! Where are you?! Akoni, come back to me!" she yelled as loudly as she could, but Akoni didn't answer. There was no sign of him anywhere.

Suddenly, Lakali felt something touch her leg. It brushed past her at first, but then she could feel watery fingers grab hold of her ankle.

"No! Please! Not again!" she screamed.

Yes, this had happened before. More of Lakali's previous dream came back to her.

She tried to look into the water to see if she could spot who it was that had a grip on her. But the water was dark, light having faded outside. There was barely even any moon, and Lakali couldn't see the beach now. All she could see was dark water around her on all sides.

Again, the watery fingers grabbed hold of her and started to pull Lakali down.

"Not again," she thought. "Please! Not again!"

But there was nothing she could do. She

couldn't fight it. She felt herself spiraling downward. Soon, she was completely underwater, finding herself unable to breathe.

Lakali jumped up from her cot and found herself gasping for breath. The dream was so real. She had never been plagued by frequent nightmares. What was happening to her?

There was something else that disturbed Lakali greatly. Even though she had initially not been able to remember what had happened during the first clear-thinking session that had gone wrong, she now remembered much of the dream that had come to her then. It was very much like the nightmare she had just had. She only had one thing to console her. At least this dream was just that, a dream and nothing more. She couldn't blame it on her clear-thinking session, or could she? Surely, the session had triggered this nightmare.

Lakali let out a sigh. She laid back down, slowly getting her breathing to a more appropriate pace.

"So much for a good night's sleep," she thought to herself.

But she knew she needed to try to go back to sleep. She just hoped she would make it through the rest of the night without any more bad dreams.

Chapter 4

The next morning, it was a busy day. Akoni was helping to make some needed repairs to one of the fishing boats. It was an old boat and had some loose boards that needed to be secured. While they were at it, they decided it was time to inspect the whole boat. A few small leaks had sprung up from time to time. They relied on their boats to bring back plenty of fish, so it was a necessary task. There were six fishing boats altogether, so the other five were manned with fishermen who had gone out to get the daily catch.

Lakali was supposed to help at the stream with washing clothes again. She was disappointed to see that none of her close friends, including Bakita, had been assigned to doing the laundry today.

Lakali was behind schedule. She had been the last one at the stream. The others had encouraged her to get back, telling her she was running out of time. But she was so close, surely she could finish if she hurried.

She had just finished the job and was headed to her hut when an intense desire came over her to go to her hut. Following the other islanders, she forgot about everything else around her and walked a little faster.

The islanders all went to their huts to take out their trinket boxes. Lakali was no different than the others. She sat on the mat on the floor of her hut and removed the lid to the box. Her eyes gazed upon the crystal inside. Soon, she was in a deep trance.

At first, the thoughts were pleasant. She saw

young children running on the beach and playing. Then, she looked out to the shoreline and saw Akoni.

"Come on! The water's perfect!" he beckoned to her.

Lakali ran barefooted eagerly through the sand. Akoni ran to meet her. They met up in the middle of the beach, the grainy sand beneath their feet. They grabbed hold of each other's hands and held their arms out in front of them. They spun around in a circle, laughing and enjoying the saltwater breeze that blew gently through their hair.

Akoni was gorgeous. Lakali couldn't believe that he was her boyfriend. How had she lucked out like this? All she wanted to do was to stay here with him forever…

Akoni was suddenly gone, nowhere to be found.

"Akoni! Akoni!" Lakali shouted frantically over and over, but there was no answer.

The other people on the beach began to fade from Lakali's vision. She was alone on the beach. As she looked around, she saw that her hut was far off in the distance. The water was no closer. All around her on all sides, she was surrounded by what appeared to be an almost-endless amount of sand.

She could feel the grains of the sand sliding around her toes, as if the ground beneath her was caving in and tumbling away from her, the sand falling to some surface far below. Suddenly, it was as if the sand formed hands. It grabbed Lakali's legs and started pulling her downward. She resisted, but it tugged on her with too great of a force.

Lakali looked below her. It was as if she could see a face and eyes in the sand. Only, it was falling away from her. As it did so, she found herself sinking faster. She was going deeper into the ground. The sand now reached up to her knees. She tried to pull herself up, but she couldn't. The more she struggled, the further down she fell.

She couldn't feel the hands on her legs anymore. The weight of the sand was enough to pull her down. It needed no help from anyone. Lakali screamed and called out for help.

"Someone! Help me! Akoni! Come help me! Please!"

She screamed loudly, but there was no one around to hear her. The sand now came to her waist. If only she had something to grab onto, then maybe she could pull herself up. But there was nothing but sand around her.

Slowly, Lakali continued to sink further into it. The sand now came to her shoulders. Her arms were completely submerged. There was no fighting it. It was best to give in to it, best not to struggle. That would only make her impending death more painful.

It was hard not to resist as the sand began to cover her head, drawing it slowly downward as if it wanted her to have plenty of time to think about the fact that she was going to die.

Oxygen... Air... Breathe... I can't...

Lakali was completely covered with sand now. There was no oxygen getting to her lungs. It wouldn't take long. Soon, she would leave this life. A fleeting thought went to Akoni.

"I'll never kiss your lips again," she thought. "I love you, Akoni. I always will."

Lakali felt herself start to tumble rapidly downward. Soon, she was thrust from the sand and landed on a hard, cold floor. The room was dark and freezing. She could hardly see.

"There you are," she heard a familiar voice.

Lakali looked up, still gasping for breath and

trying to cough out the sand from her mouth. In the dark room, she could barely see the man who stood over her.

"Akoni!" she cried.

She tried to get to her feet, but she was unsteady. Akoni reached down and pulled her to her feet.

"There you go," he said.

"Oh, Akoni! I thought I'd never see you again!" she sobbed. "Hold me and don't ever let go."

She threw her arms around him and clung to him tightly.

"I've got you," Akoni said coldly. "You're not going anywhere."

Lakali suddenly felt a strange distance between them even though Akoni had his arms wrapped around her. She tried to pull away, but Akoni was too strong. He wasn't letting go of her.

"Don't struggle," Akoni said. "It'll be easier if you don't struggle."

"Akoni, what are you doing?" Lakali asked frantically, still trying to free herself to no avail. "Let me go!"

"I can't do as you request," Akoni replied. "I must follow instructions. Please. Remain calm. Everything will work out. Just wait and see."

Lakali's heart was racing. What was going on? Why was Akoni acting like this, and why was he being so mysterious?

"Let me go! Now!" Lakali screamed.

Akoni said nothing as he held onto her even more tightly. Her head was resting against his shoulder. She couldn't see his face anymore.

"I thought you loved me," she said. "Please let me go."

"I see you have the girl now," a voice sounded from across the room.

"Yes. I've done as you instructed," Akoni replied.

"Tie her up to that post over there," the voice commanded.

"Will do," Akoni answered and dragged Lakali to a wooden post that stood in the middle of the room.

He pulled her arms behind her and began tying her to the pole. She tried to pull away from him, but he was too strong.

"Please, Akoni! Don't do this!" Lakali begged. "You're not thinking clearly."

"Of course I'm thinking clearly," Akoni replied. "I always think clearly. The sessions make sure of that. They help me to make wise decisions like I'm doing right now, following the instructions of our benevolent leaders."

"I don't understand," Lakali cried. "What do they want from me?"

"I don't know," Akoni answered. "They haven't told me that much. I only do what I'm told."

"Please, Akoni. Listen to me," Lakali begged. "You don't want to do this. You love me."

"I love our wise and benevolent leaders," Akoni replied. "They only want what is best for us."

Lakali couldn't stop crying. It was useless. There was no getting through to Akoni.

"Have you done as we instructed?" the voice asked.

"I have," Akoni answered. "The girl is secured."

"The girl?" Lakali asked angrily. "Is that what you're calling me?"

"You are a girl, aren't you?" Akoni inquired. "It's an appropriate thing to call you."

"I'm Lakali! I have a name. Use it!" Lakali shouted angrily.

"The girl is secured," Akoni repeated.

"What's happening?" Lakali asked, more frightened than ever. "I don't understand. This doesn't make any sense."

"Come and retrieve the object, and we will tell you what to do," the voice instructed Akoni.

He left Lakali alone in the darkness. Now, she could begin to hear other sounds around her. They were the sounds of men and women screaming. Even though no one was close to her, the sounds were terrifying. What was happening to those people? Better yet, what was going to happen to her? She was afraid she was going to find out way too soon.

Lakali could hear footsteps. Akoni was wearing some shoes with a hard sole. That was unusual. He was usually either barefoot or wearing sturdy sandals. Each sound echoed as his foot stepped across the hard floor. Soon, Lakali could feel him standing directly in front of her.

A small sliver of light came in from the ceiling, just enough to illuminate the space around her. She could see Akoni clearly now.

"Akoni, please!" Lakali pleaded. "Whatever they asked you to do, don't do it!"

"Lakali," Akoni said.

"Yes, I'm Lakali, your girlfriend," she replied.

"I love you?" he asked, as if it was a question.

"Yes, you love me," she replied, trying desperately to get through to him.

Again, she heard the screams of men and women in the distance.

"Please, don't hurt me!" Lakali begged.

"I would never hurt you," Akoni replied. "The leaders do not want to hurt us. They only want what is best for us."

Slowly, he raised the steely blade up so that

Lakali could clearly see it.

"What's that?!" she asked nervously.

"What it looks like," Akoni answered. "Please, stand still. I'll make it quick. I wouldn't want to hurt you."

"Akoni, no!" Lakali sobbed.

"I have to," Akoni replied. "I must do what the leaders ask. Close your eyes and just relax."

"I can't," Lakali cried. "I can't look away."

The worst part of knowing that she was going to die was knowing that it was going to be by Akoni's hand.

Slowly, Akoni moved the steel blade to Lakali's throat. She could feel the cold metal pressing against her neck.

"You don't have to do this, Akoni," she tried one last time.

"Shhh..." Akoni said as he pressed the knife harder against her skin.

Lakali could feel the blade beginning to tear at her skin. She felt herself going cold, ice-cold. It was as if her life had already left her. Lakali felt the tears rolling down her face. She wouldn't even get to kiss Akoni goodbye.

Everything was spinning in the room around her. Lakali was again confused, sitting on her mat. What had just happened? Was this another nightmare, or were the strange memories supposed to be some sort of a warning?

That was crazy. Akoni would never do anything so hideous, and she knew that their leaders would never authorize it. Surely, it was just another nightmare that was being caused by the clear-thinking sessions. Lakali knew one thing. She definitely didn't want to go to the leaders and tell them about the nightmare she had just had! They would think she was crazy for sure, and they would also be angry that she had thought so poorly of them even if it had only been in a dream.

Lakali put the trinket box away and got up from the mat, still unsteady on her feet. She stepped outside of the hut, thinking that some fresh air might do her some good. She saw Akoni coming out of his hut. A cold chill ran up her spine.

Akoni...

It was as if she could still feel the cold steel blade against her throat, hungrily tearing into her skin.

"Get ahold of yourself," she thought silently. "It was just a nightmare. Nothing more. Akoni loves you. He would never hurt you."

"I've got to go finish a couple of things we didn't quite finish this morning, things that can't wait until tomorrow," Akoni called to her. "I won't be gone long."

Lakali waved to him.

"Okay," she answered as enthusiastically as she could. "Don't be long. There isn't much more light left in the day."

"I know," Akoni replied. "I promise to hurry."

Lakali didn't mind that Akoni didn't have time to come see her. She knew that it was all in her head, but she was having trouble forgetting the disturbing images.

Lakali put on her swimsuit and went out for a swim.

It wasn't until dinner that Akoni came back.

"I'm sorry. I didn't mean to be gone that long," he said. "We found more repairs than we thought we would, and we want to get all of the boats operating again as soon as possible."

"It's okay. I understand," Lakali replied.

She had been okay with not seeing Akoni anymore that day. Even though she knew it had only been a dream, she was still disturbed by it. Even now, several hours later, she couldn't forget about it.

When they were done eating, they walked off to be by themselves and sat down on the beach. There was no one in earshot.

"Akoni, would you ever hurt me?" Lakali asked.

"What kind of question is that?" Akoni replied. "Of course I would never hurt you!"

"What if the leaders asked you to?" Lakali inquired, immediately regretting her question.

"What?! Lakali, why would you even ask such a crazy thing?!" Akoni inquired.

"It's nothing. I'm sorry," she said. "It was just a weird thought."

"Well, it's a thought that no one else needs to hear about, and certainly not our leaders!" Akoni replied. "They wouldn't be happy to have you talking about them like that."

"I didn't mean it," Lakali insisted. "I just get weird thoughts sometimes."

"That worries me," Akoni said. "It seems to me that you aren't getting as much out of your clear-thinking sessions as you should. If that's the case, then we should seek the leaders' help. I would leave out your preposterous question, though."

"No, we don't need to do that," Lakali assured him. "I know they would never ask you to hurt me. I just wanted to know that you would protect me, no matter what. It wasn't like I expected them to actually do such a thing! That would be impossible!"

Akoni looked at Lakali skeptically. He still wasn't convinced that it was a random question.

"Really," Lakali insisted. "I won't ask anything like that again."

"Please don't," Akoni replied. "It makes me

nervous for you to say such a thing."

"I promise," Lakali assured him. "Can we just sit here and enjoy being with each other? Let's have no more talk about going to the leaders for help. We're both fine."

"Okay," Akoni agreed.

But he was determined to keep a close eye on Lakali. Sometimes, he really worried about her.

Chapter 5

Akoni laid on the cot in his hut unable to move, frozen with fear. He stared intently at the man standing in his doorway, his eerie glowing green eyes watching him. In the darkness, Akoni didn't know if the man could see that he was awake or not. He didn't know what the man wanted. Why was he just standing there like that, watching him? And what was with those eyes? They were like nothing Akoni had ever seen before. Had he seen the eyes without the man's face and body attached, he would have never guessed that those eyes belonged to any human on the island. Yet, there the man was, undeniable and as real as Akoni had ever been.

As Akoni stared back at the strange eyes, an odd feeling began to come over him. The air was getting thick, and it was becoming harder to breathe. It was almost as if the man in the doorway was somehow sucking the oxygen slowly out of the room. Akoni panicked and opened his mouth to breathe in as much air as possible. But the more he struggled to find the oxygen, the harder it was to come by.

He felt his throat constricting. It was as if invisible hands were upon it. He grasped for his throat and tried to pull the hands away, but there was no one there. He thought about getting out of bed and rushing the man in the doorway. If he shoved him backwards, maybe he could run outside and get some fresh air. But he couldn't bring himself to do it. It was as if he was being held down. He felt paralyzed and couldn't move an inch.

In the dark corners of the room, Akoni could

hear a familiar voice calling to him. It belonged to Lakali.

"Don't trust him!" she called to Akoni. "Whatever you do, do not trust the man in the doorway!"

Akoni didn't trust the man standing at his door. He didn't need the obvious stated, but he knew Lakali was in some way trying to help. It didn't matter. Akoni was helpless. He couldn't move, and the air was being taken from his lungs. There was little oxygen left in the room now. Combined with the ever-tightening grip on his throat, Akoni felt himself start to black out. He fought to stay awake, but he couldn't stop the darkness from beginning to overcome him.

As he felt his final breath leaving him, he heard Lakali again. Only this time, she was no longer speaking. Instead, she was laughing loudly and hysterically.

"I told you so!" her voice sounded from across the room.

It was so loud that it bounced off the walls and drove itself right into Akoni's heart.

Akoni awoke from his clear-thinking session with a start. He found his heart was racing, and he was breathing rapidly with his mouth open. It took him a moment to get his bearings. Finally, he realized where he was and began to slow his breathing. He remembered nothing of the session itself, no memories of the horrifying thoughts he had just encountered. He had never awoken from the sessions in such a way before. It took Akoni by surprise. He didn't know what to make of it. Was there something wrong with him? Was the session not successful? He knew that if he continued to struggle like this as he came out of the sessions, he would have to go to the leaders and ask for help.

Chapter 6

Lakali screamed and pulled her legs tightly to her chest. She swatted outward with her hands wildly, trying to get the creatures away from her. She was surrounded on all sides. There was no escape. In front of her, slithering toward her were venomous snakes. To her right side were large, hairy tarantulas. On her other side were large scary-looking insects. Behind her was the wall of her hut. Lakali suddenly lost her footing and fell to the floor. She used her arms to pull herself backward, trying to get away from the army of deadly creatures that was still descending on her.

"Oh, no!" she thought as she reached the wall of the hut.

There was now nowhere else to go. Even if she could pull herself up, the only way to the door would mean walking barefoot across the tarantulas, and Lakali was terrified of spiders.

Lakali pulled herself into a sitting position. She sat there with her back against the wall of the hut, shaking and crying. She screamed for Akoni to come help her, but no one came. She was on her own.

There was a stick on the ground near her. She knew her biggest threat was from the snakes. If even one snake bit her and injected its venom, she would die within minutes. These snakes were some of the deadliest serpents on the island. Lakali used the stick and swung it around, but especially in front of her since that was where the snakes were. She waved it wildly, trying to distract the slithering beasts and other creatures from coming near her.

But it didn't seem to make any difference. Everything was closing in on her. Lakali couldn't pull her legs up any tighter. There was nowhere left to retreat to. And yet, the snakes kept approaching, slithering closer and closer.

As she sobbed and screamed, Lakali's attention was too diverted by the snakes and tarantulas, and she lost track of where the bugs were. She began to feel them crawling up her body and sinking their teeth and stingers into her skin. She jumped up and tried wildly to knock them off. In doing so, she lost the stick on the floor in front of her and the snakes temporarily scattered. She brushed several bugs off of her, but some had crawled underneath her clothing on her back. She frantically started to remove her halter top, but she was distracted when she felt the large tarantulas crawling up her right leg.

Lakali screamed even louder and shook her leg. She tried desperately to get the tarantulas off. But they clung to her, and more kept coming. Horrified, she saw that she had about a dozen tarantulas crawling up her leg. Meanwhile, a hundred or more bugs were crawling up her left side, and many bugs had already wedged themselves between her clothing and her skin.

Lakali jumped around and swatted wildly at the bugs and tarantulas, finally losing her footing again and falling onto the floor once more. The snakes saw their opportunity and slithered over her, encasing her body with their great numbers. Lakali couldn't move. She was at the mercy of the beasts upon her. By now, the only part of her body that didn't have any creatures on it was her face. She tried to steady her breathing, but she could barely breathe.

She saw it come closer, stretching out its

body above her head and pointing its triangular face downward, leaning its face over hers. Lakali screamed as the snake lunged forward, striking her on her cheek. Lakali could feel her heartrate increase and knew she only had seconds left to live. She gave one last thought to Akoni and regretted that she would never kiss his lips again.

Lakali sat on her mat with the trinket box in her lap. She was grasping it with all of her strength, her fingernails almost digging into the sides of the box. She was breathing rapidly and was hyperventilating. She could still sense the bugs, snakes and tarantulas around her. She dropped the box and jumped up, turning around in circles as she removed her clothing and looked for any bugs that might still be on her skin.

Discovering the bugs were gone, she reached up and felt her face, feeling for the puncture wound left by the snake, but she found that it also was no longer there. Slowly, she began to realize that the memories weren't real but were again left over from her clear-thinking session.

Lakali was exhausted both physically and mentally. These horrible memories and dreams were too much. Was there no way to stop them? Was she always going to be plagued by them? The thought was too much. Then, an even more frightening thought came to her. Were these dreams meant to warn her about something? Lakali again saw Akoni standing in front of her, a knife pressed against her throat. She could almost feel the steel blade against her skin as she recalled the terrifying dream.

It was all ridiculous. She knew in her heart that Akoni would never do anything like that, not even if the leaders asked him to. She also knew that the leaders would never ask him to do such a thing anyway. Why would they? There would be no reason for them to want her dead. The leaders looked out for the islanders. She had always respected them.

Even so, something was wrong. Lakali knew it. Should she go to the leaders? Should she tell them about all of the crazy dreams that she was having? Maybe if she left out the fact that they were coming to her in her clear-thinking sessions, then she could tell them. Maybe they could help her. No, she couldn't go to them. Something still told her that was a bad idea.

But she had to figure this out. Somehow, she had to make sense of it all because deep down, Lakali felt like both she and Akoni were in danger. But from what? None of this made any sense.

The knock on the door startled Lakali. She took a deep breath. The nightmare was all over now. She didn't need to be afraid anymore. That's what she tried to tell herself.

There was a second knock. Lakali started to walk to the door when she realized that she was still without clothing, having pulled her garments off frantically when she thought her body was covered in bugs. She picked up her clothes, once more checking them to make sure there truly were no bugs or spiders in them. Seeing they were safe, she got dressed again.

Lakali opened the door and saw Akoni standing there, smiling. Somehow, he had pushed away the feeling of thinking there was something wrong with him and was no longer worried about his odd session. A peacefulness had come over him, and he knew that the clear-thinking sessions were working exactly as they were supposed to.

"I don't have to work this afternoon," he said. "Do you want to go for a swim in the ocean?"

Lakali had a flashback to her dreams about being in the ocean. She felt herself shiver.

"Swimming?" she asked with unwanted trepidation sounding in her voice.

"Yeah," Akoni replied. "I know it's one of your favorite things to do. Are you alright? You seem off, like something's bothering you. It took you a long time to answer the door again. Is something wrong?"

Lakali wasn't alright. Who would be if they kept having the kinds of dreams that she was having? To top it off, she couldn't get today's nightmare out of her mind. She still felt like bugs were crawling on her, but she didn't want Akoni to suspect that anything was wrong. Something told her that it was best if he didn't know about the nightmares and what was happening to her in the clear-thinking sessions.

"I'm fine," she lied. "A swim sounds like a good idea. Give me a few minutes?"

Her voice wasn't super convincing. As much as Akoni wanted to find out what was bothering her, he still sensed that he needed to let it go. If he pushed the subject any further, it would only upset her more. He knew Lakali. She did things on her own time. He hoped he would eventually find out what kept upsetting her. But for now, he had to try to be patient. She would tell him when she was ready.

"No problem," he said, trying to hide his worry. "Just come out and meet me when you're ready."

"Okay," Lakali said.

"Don't be long," Akoni urged.

"I won't," Lakali replied.

She closed the door and went to sit down on the cot. She needed a few moments to clear her head. Still remembering the horrible memories of her clear-thinking session, she drew her feet up to the cot and looked at the floor, wanting to make sure there was truly nothing there.

Why was this happening to her? Why was she suddenly having all of these bad dreams? The leaders told them that the sessions would make them think clearly and help them make wise decisions. Did good decision-making come from having these nightmares? But they weren't really nightmares. They were different somehow. Lakali knew that something had gone wrong with her clear-thinking sessions. Whatever the problem was, it was causing the bad dreams. A pattern was developing with each day bringing a new one. Daymares... That's what she would call them.

Lakali wondered for a moment if she should tell Akoni. She wanted so desperately to have someone to talk to. Akoni loved her. He would want to help. But she knew what he would suggest. He would say that she needed to go to the leaders. Lakali couldn't risk that. No, she couldn't tell anyone what was happening, not even Akoni.

As Lakali sat on the cot, she tried to remember more. She could sense that there was something missing, something that she wasn't remembering. She thought back to what she had been doing prior to the clear-thinking session. She had been on the beach in front of her hut, working with some dough, getting it ready to bake in the sun oven. Lakali tried to concentrate. If she focused hard enough, maybe she could remember more. She closed her eyes and tried to block everything else out. She pictured herself sitting in the sand, kneading the dough. Lakali's mind was stronger than the other islanders. As she concentrated, the memory started to come back.

She had been kneading the dough when suddenly, an intense feeling of urgency came over her. She knew she must go to her hut right away and open her trinket box. She put the dough down and got up, walking toward her hut. She could see from her side vision that other islanders were feeling the same urgency and were hurrying to get to their huts to open their trinket boxes also.

Lakali's mind suddenly went to another place and time. It was as if she had finally been able to break through the barrier that was keeping her from recalling the memories.

Lakali saw herself as a young child. A similar feeling came over her, much like the feeling that had come over her today. She knew that she had something urgent to tend to. She had been with Caristiona on the beach. They had been playing tag. Both she and her best friend stopped what they were doing. They followed the other children and young teens who were all headed to the south.

None of them had received their trinket boxes yet. While the other islanders went to their clear-thinking sessions, the young islanders were all beckoned by a sound that only they could hear. It was a joyful sound that called to them, and they had a great desire to obey. There was no defiance. Everyone wanted to follow the sound. Even the young children who were unable to walk on their own also wanted to go to it. As soon as they were old enough to do so, they happily followed the call of the sound just like all the others.

Together, they all went to a large playground that was surrounded by tall wooden fences. Entranced by the happy musical sounds that filled their ears and took their thoughts away from anything but gathering at the playground, they never questioned it when one of the leaders came and closed the gate behind them.

Once there, the children and young teens retreated to themselves, finding places on swings or under trees. Their minds were filled with joyful thoughts, and there was no place they would rather be. Shortly, they would be playing with each other and have no thoughts of anything happening outside of the playground.

When the islanders received their trinket boxes, the memories of their time on the playground quickly faded. Within a few weeks, no memories would remain. Entranced by their own need to go to their trinket boxes, no one gave a second thought as to where the children were or what they were doing. Because they had forgotten about going to the playground, no one spoke of it. The children didn't speak of it either. After the clear-thinking sessions were over, the children were released from the playground. Within minutes, they forgot about where they had been and what they had been doing.

Lakali was remembering it quite clearly now, though. She remembered how happy she had felt and how peaceful the playground had been. Why had she forgotten about it? It had been such a wonderful time for her. Why couldn't that peaceful feeling last? Instead, she was now plagued with terrifying thoughts. The happy childhood memories seemed so distant, so far gone from her current life.

Lakali opened her eyes. She found herself taking several deep breaths, slowly inhaling and exhaling. It was such a long time ago. Was she the only one who remembered the playground? She knew she would have to talk to Akoni about it later. She had to know if he remembered it or not.

Still, there was something she wasn't remembering, another piece to the mystery of her clear-thinking sessions. She knew Akoni was waiting for her, but he would have to wait a few minutes more. She had to think back to what had happened earlier. She closed her eyes, making one more attempt to remember.

She could now feel it again, the intense urgency that had come over her. Lakali had ignored the other islanders and continued walking toward her hut. She walked inside and picked up the trinket box, then taking her place on the mat.

The box was so pretty and now had a hypnotic effect on her. She couldn't think of anything else. Nothing else mattered except for the box. As she sat down, she held the box in her lap. Gently with her right hand, she opened the lid. That was when she saw it. It was funny how she had thought of it as ordinary and had never noticed how beautiful it really was. Inside the box was the most beautiful shiny and sparkly clear crystal that she had ever seen. Inside the crystal, beautifully-colored dots shone out at her. The colors were bright and vivid. They included pink, green, lavender, and silver.

Lakali sat as if glued to her mat, mesmerized by the colors and the lights that sprang out from the box. The crystal lit up the whole room as a soft white light encased her. It was the most blissful feeling that she had ever felt, even more peaceful than what she had felt on the playground.

Slowly, Lakali felt her eyes start to close. At first, the thoughts that went through her mind were gentle. Butterflies floating on the breeze, birds flying overhead, kittens meowing and rubbing against her legs.

But then, the light gave way to a darkness that slowly crept over her. The room went black. Even though she could feel herself tensing up and wanting to leave, she still felt glued to the mat. She couldn't move now even if her life depended on it. That was when her daymare had begun. She could see the line of bugs making their way into her hut.

They marched past her and made their way to her left side. Then, the tarantulas made their entrance, taking their place on her right side. When they were all in their spots, the snakes began slithering in through her doorway.

Lakali opened her eyes and was gasping for breath. She was breathing much too quickly and was hyperventilating again. It was as if she had just had the daymare all over again.

Frantically, Lakali looked around and saw that the hut was clear. Slowly, Lakali got her breathing under control. She closed her eyes again, but not because she wanted to remember anything more. She had had enough memories for one day! Lakali took slow, deep breaths as she forced herself to think of happy things like sunning herself on the beach. Once she felt calm enough, she opened her eyes and thought about her memories. What did they all mean?

Lakali got up slowly. She walked over to the trinket box. She didn't know if she could do this or not. There was a strict rule that no islander was to ever open their trinket box unless it was during a clear-thinking session. If she got caught, she would be taken to the leaders immediately and would receive a harsh punishment.

What if Akoni caught her? Would he turn her in, or would he look the other way? How much did he love her? Was it enough to keep him from his obligations to the leaders? Lakali again saw him standing in front of her, a sharp steel knife pressed against her throat.

"No! Pull yourself together!" Lakali found herself speaking aloud.

She didn't have time for this. Akoni was waiting for her. She had to push the bad memories and doubts about Akoni out of her thoughts. She needed to do this, and she needed to be quick about it.

Lakali walked to the door and double-checked to see that it was tightly closed. When she was sure no one could see her, she walked back to the trinket box.

She wondered if the leaders would know what she was about to do. Did they have some way of knowing what she was doing even if no eyes were watching her at the moment? She didn't know, but she also knew that she couldn't keep having these daymares and not try to figure out why. They were destroying her. One way or another, she had to know what was going on.

She picked up the trinket box and sat down in her rocking chair. She held it on her lap for several minutes before getting up the nerve to open it. With her right hand, she lifted the lid and looked into the box. She saw the crystal, but it looked different now. She had seen the crystal before, having caught glimpses of it as she came out of her clear-thinking sessions and spotting it briefly as she closed the box. There didn't seem to be anything special about it from what she saw in those moments. It looked like an ordinary crystal, clear and devoid of life.

She looked at it more closely now. As she examined it, she could see that it wasn't completely clear. Instead, she could barely see hints of colors within the crystal. They were hard to spot. But if she looked at the crystal closely, the colors were there. It didn't matter that the crystal wasn't shining at the moment. She could still see them.

Lakali cautiously put her right hand in the box and removed the crystal, half-expecting to be killed instantly for even touching it. When nothing happened, she held the crystal in her hand and turned it around, inspecting all of its sides. It looked so harmless now. There was nothing sinister about it. Yet, somehow, Lakali knew that it held some sort of power and that it was responsible for her daymares. She thought about hiding it, but she was afraid. If anyone ever found out that she had removed the crystal, she was afraid of what the leaders might do to her. Taking a deep breath and releasing it, she placed the crystal back in the box and put the box back on the shelf. She returned to the rocking chair and tried to make sense of it all, but she kept coming up blank.

Lakali heard another knock on the door.

"Are you coming?" Akoni was becoming impatient.

"Yeah," Lakali answered. "I'll be right there! I promise!"

She quickly slipped on her bathing suit and went outside, meeting Akoni. He looked at her in her bikini and smiled.

"Maybe the beach was a bad idea," he said. "We could go inside instead."

"You wanted to go for a swim," Lakali replied. "So, we're going for a swim."

Right then, the last place she wanted to be was in her hut or anywhere near that crystal!

Lakali walked past Akoni and headed toward the beach, leaving him behind. Akoni watched her, once more knowing that something was wrong. She was being distant again. He let out a sigh and followed her to the beach where they spent the next hour swimming and playing in the waves. As much as Lakali wanted to talk to Akoni about her memories, she refrained from doing so. She needed more time to think about everything. For now, she focused on trying to convince Akoni that she was fine.

When Akoni tired of splashing water on her, he drew Lakali to him. He reached over and kissed her, but Lakali didn't return his kiss as enthusiastically as she usually did. Her mind was too preoccupied.

Again, Akoni wanted to ask her what was wrong, but he decided it was best to let her have some space. If this went on for too long, he would have to say something. Maybe she was just tired. Perhaps she had had too much sun.

Lakali wanted nothing more than to get her mind off of her troubles. She would have loved to have gotten lost in Akoni's kiss and let the bad memories slip away from her, but she knew she couldn't do that. She knew that she must hold onto the memories, and she must remember everything about the crystal also. Somehow, she knew it was important to not forget about it. Whatever she did, she must remember always!

Chapter 7

Lakali didn't get much sleep that night. She tossed and turned most of the night, but she was at least grateful that she didn't have any bad dreams. She had been assigned to meal preparation for the day. That meant she would be really busy. Everyone was accustomed to a quick breakfast, usually some fruit like bananas or papayas and some bread that had been baked the day before. They would take breaks from their work shifts to get a hearty lunch, though. It would be a quick meal, everyone anxious to return to their jobs to get them done as quickly as possible. There would be plenty of time for socializing with the other islanders at dinner.

It was the responsibility of those on meal preparation duty to make sure that there was plenty to eat in the dining hut. People would come in at different times, depending on what jobs they were doing. There needed to be enough food there as early as ten o'clock for the people who had started work early in the morning.

Akoni had to head out early also. Otherwise, he would have regretted that Lakali had to leave for her shift so soon.

Tired or not, Lakali had a job to do. She threw on her clothes and headed out to start cooking the meat and boiling the vegetables. It was a lot of work, but at least there were always several women assigned to the job.

Sometimes when she was working with meal preparation, Lakali would see Akoni briefly when he came in for lunch. Today, she didn't get see him. He had come in for lunch while she was peeling more potatoes for the workers who would be coming in later.

Lakali was so busy that she barely had time to think about her worries. She had a brief moment of panic when she started cutting the vegetables, though. Looking at the steel blade that she was using to slice the yellow squash, she couldn't help but have an unwanted flashback, again feeling the sharpness of the blade Akoni was holding pressed against her throat.

She wouldn't allow herself to fall apart. She pulled herself together and focused on the work at hand, glad when the current task was done. She would much rather be tending to the cooking and taking the food to the dining hut than working with the knife!

It was a relief when her work shift was over. She was exhausted. She and the other ladies had also been working on dinner. They would come back and finish later after the clear-thinking session, whenever that was. No one knew for sure when it would be, so it was best to get as much done for dinner as they could before finishing their morning shift. While they couldn't start cooking dinner yet, they could have all of the vegetables prepared and ready to go. That would make finishing dinner a lot easier. By then, everyone would be really tired. They would be glad that they had done as much prep work as possible ahead of time.

At least, the women who prepared meals worked near their huts. That would be convenient when it came time for the clear-thinking session.

Of course, the women were allotted some time for breaks throughout the day. Lakali had been working hard and was tired. She told the others that she was going to take a break. No one timed anyone when they took their breaks. Everyone trusted that when people were rested enough, they would return to their work. Of course, there were occasional times when others got irritated, thinking someone had been gone too long.

Lakali decided to go sit on the beach for a while. She wondered where Akoni was. Surely, he was back from his morning shift. He was probably in his hut, but Lakali wanted to be alone. So, she didn't bother to go to look for him. He had been delayed, though, and had gotten back later than he had meant to. He was barely returning when he saw her walking toward the shore.

"Lakali!" he called.

Lakali turned to face him. He came to meet her.

"I'm going to help Amzi with something," he said.

"What? Did you just get back?" Lakali asked.

There was no one close enough to pay any attention to them.

"Yeah, I lost track of time," Akoni confessed.

"You'd better be more careful next time," Lakali replied.

"I know, but it's okay," Akoni answered. "We lost track of time, but the clear-thinking session hasn't happened yet. No one will be upset."

"You'll still be near?" Lakali asked.

"Yeah, we'll be in his hut," Akoni answered. "He has a chair with a broken leg. I'm going to help him fix it."

"That's good," Lakali replied. "You're a good friend."

"I try to be," Akoni replied. "I'm sorry I can't stay with you, though. I know you'll be busy later with dinner."

"It's okay," Lakali said. "I understand."

Akoni gave her a quick kiss.

"I've got to go," he lamented. "Think clearly in your session!"

"You too," Lakali said, thinking that was the last thing she would be doing.

Lakali watched him leave. She didn't mind that he had something to do. She just needed a few moments by herself. Maybe if she sat and relaxed on the sand, she could clear her head. Maybe she could figure out what to do about her clear-thinking sessions. She had barely sat down on the sand, though, when she felt a sudden urge to go to her trinket box.

"No," Lakali said to herself. "I won't do it. I won't!"

But the pull on her was too great. She felt herself becoming nervous and shaky. She couldn't stay away from it. She got up reluctantly, trying to will herself to stay on the beach. She stood there for a few moments, trying to resist the temptation. She watched the last of the islanders enter their hut. Just the fact that she was still standing here and watching them showed that she could be strong enough to resist. Didn't it?

Lakali's heart started to race. She started breathing much too quickly. It was as if someone's imaginary hands had grabbed hold of her and were pulling her toward the hut.

"I don't want to," she found herself saying aloud in a low voice, but no one could hear her. The other islanders were already inside their huts now. "Please, no!"

"You must," an inner voice told Lakali. "You cannot resist. Do as you have been told to do."

Reluctantly, Lakali headed toward her hut. Her feet started walking toward it even though she tried desperately to stop them. It was as if she didn't have any control over her own body.

Lakali walked into the hut and took the trinket box from the shelf. She then found herself on the mat on the floor. She held the box in her lap. Her eyes were now fixed on it. She wanted desperately to look away, but she couldn't. Even so, she was resisting the temptation of the box more than any other islander had ever been able to do.

Slowly, Lakali opened the lid and looked upon the crystal. It was so beautiful. It quickly put her in a trance.

At first, the thoughts were peaceful. She heard birds chirping and looked up to see them flying from branch to branch in the trees above her. In reality, her eyes were still on the crystal, but all she could see were the trees around her.

"It's beautiful," she said. "The perfect paradise."

Lakali savored the moment. She breathed in the fresh island air and observed all the beauty around her.

Then, she heard a distant voice. It seemed familiar. Who was that? She knew she should know who it was, but she couldn't quite place who it was.

"Lakali," the voice spoke.

It was coming from deeper within the trees, far in the distance. Lakali started walking away from the huts and the beach. She kept going until she was surrounded by nothing but tall island trees. Many of them were palm trees, holding plenty of coconuts, papayas and bananas for the islanders. However, there were some island pine trees and island oak trees also. Where Lakali was, they all seemed to grow together.

"Lakali," the voice called to her again.

This time, it was louder and sounded more urgent. Again, Lakali was sure she should recognize the owner of the voice. But somehow, it eluded her, almost as if it didn't want her to know who it was.

"Who are you?" Lakali shouted. "Where are you? What do you want?"

"Lakali, it's me," the voice called louder.

She recognized the voice now. How could she not have recognized it before?

"Lakali! Help me!"

The voice was now frantic, and Lakali heard Akoni screaming at the top of his lungs. He was terrified. Something was wrong. He was in trouble. She had to get to him!

"I'm coming!" Lakali called desperately. "Don't go anywhere! I'm coming!"

"Lakali! Hurry! You're going to be too late! Help me!" Akoni shouted.

Again, his call for help was followed by several terrified screams.

Lakali ran for all she was worth, going deeper among the trees and always finding that no matter how far she went, she seemed to not be getting any closer to Akoni. In fact, his voice seemed to drift further away from her. She could barely hear him at all.

"Akoni!" she shouted. "Where did you go?!"

"You're too late," she heard Akoni say.

His voice was very distant now.

"Goodbye, Lakali."

There was an intense sadness to Akoni's voice. It was as if he was telling her that she would never see him again.

"No, Akoni. No!" Lakali shouted.

Then, she broke down crying and collapsed to the ground. She put her head down on her lap and let herself cry.

"I love you, Akoni," she sobbed. "I always will."

There was suddenly a loud thunderous sound

above her, followed by a dark sinister laugh that filled the air all around her. The wind picked up and started blowing furiously. Lakali found that it was hard to even sit on the ground. She felt like the wind was going to topple her over if it didn't pick her up and carry her away.

She tried to get to her feet, but the wind was so strong that it kept knocking her down. She crawled to the nearest tree. It was a tall palm tree. She tried to grasp onto it to try to use it as leverage to pull herself up. She wrapped her arms around it and held herself there as if she was hanging on for dear life.

Was this what a hurricane would feel like? Lakali had never experienced one for real, but she remembered Bakita telling about how one had hit the island back when their ancestors had first arrived. Fortunately, they weren't really common on the island. Lakali never wanted to see what one was like, but she now wondered if this was indeed a hurricane that had descended upon her.

Again, a sinister laugh came from overhead. As she looked around, Lakali noticed that the trees didn't look normal anymore. It was as if their trunks had faces. She could see the eyes looking at her and could see their mouths move as the laughing grew louder. It was as if all the trees had come together in a chorus of laughter, only there wasn't anything funny about it.

"What do you want?!" Lakali screamed. "What do you need me to do?!"

More laughter surrounded her, along with several claps of loud thunder. The wind grabbed hold of Lakali and pulled her from the tree that she was still clinging to. She felt herself flying through the air and going between trees. She dodged their branches which were now arms as they reached out, trying to snatch her from her unwanted flight.

"Help me!" Lakali tried to scream, but it was hard to get the words out. She could barely even catch her breath as she was flying with the wind.

Suddenly, the wind stopped and Lakali was flung violently to the ground. She noticed an incredible pain in her leg and looked down in horror to see that her right leg was broken.

The trees picked up their roots and started walking toward her. They surrounded her in a circle and stood towering over her. Some of them removed branches and started throwing them down on her while others removed their fruit and pummeled her with coconuts and papayas.

Lakali was in an intense amount of pain. She knew she could never get away. She would die here. Then, one of the coconuts hit her on the head so hard that she blacked out. As expected, this was going to become her grave.

Lakali came to her senses. Once again, she was hyperventilating. She looked down at the trinket box that was still on her lap. Another daymare... Of course. That's all it was. Lakali watched as the last little flicker of colored light from the crystal faded. Even so, she was seeing more now than she had ever seen before, at least as far as she could remember. Normally, she couldn't remember the colors at all. Somehow, Lakali knew that she had pulled herself out of her daymare sooner than she was supposed to, if only by a few seconds. Did that mean she was getting stronger? Would she find a way to be able to stop the daymares altogether?

It wasn't long before there was a knock on the door. Akoni... Naturally. He always wanted to see her right after the clear-thinking sessions. It had never annoyed her before, but she wanted to be alone. She couldn't pull herself together. There was no time to recover from one daymare before another one came. Lakali didn't think she could hide the fact that she was upset. Her hands were shaking. This was becoming a common thing after a clear-thinking session. Seeing her like this, Akoni would worry about her. He would want her to go to the leaders. He would think they could help. He hadn't had time to fix that chair. Maybe she could get him to go away.

Lakali had to admit that she even sometimes wondered if she should go to the leaders, but some internal instinct kept her from being able to do so. She knew she had to figure out more about what was happening before she went to see them. Maybe, eventually, they could help. But for right now, Lakali knew that she was on her own.

"Lakali!" Akoni called to her from the other side of the door. "Are you alright?"

Still shaken from her daymare, Lakali reluctantly put the trinket box back in its position and got up from the mat. She walked to the door and saw Akoni's worried face.

"You used to come right out after the sessions," he greeted her. "Now, I have to come get you every day. This isn't like you, Lakali. Please tell me what's bothering you."

"It's nothing," Lakali replied, but her voice wasn't convincing.

"Lakali, I've been trying to not say anything," Akoni said. "But I can see that something is wrong. Does it have to do with the clear-thinking sessions?"

"No! Of course not!" Lakali lied. "I've just not been sleeping well at night."

"Are you ill?" Akoni asked. "Do we need to let the leaders know? Perhaps they could give you something to make you sleep better."

"No!" Lakali nearly shouted. "I don't want you

to do that! You have to promise me."

"It's okay. I won't," Akoni said. "We all get insomnia from time to time. I'm sure that's all it is. I just don't want it to go on for too long."

"It won't," Lakali assured him. "I'm sure of it."

"I still need to go help Amzi. We have a little work to do on the fishing boats first. I was hoping I'd have time to fix the chair before the clear-thinking session. Now, it looks like I'm going to be busy all day," Akoni lamented.

"It's okay. I have to go back to finish preparing dinner anyway," Lakali said. "Since the clear-thinking session happened as early as it did, I have a little time free before I have to go back to work."

"That's good," Akoni replied. "Go back to bed. Use that time to get some rest. You need it."

Lakali nodded.

"I think you're right," she said.

"Are you sure you're going to be okay?" Akoni asked.

"I promise. Just promise me you won't talk to anyone else about this. No one!" Lakali said.

"I promise," Akoni replied. "I wouldn't do anything to upset you. You know I would do anything to help you. All you have to do is ask."

"I know," Lakali replied. "And I appreciate it. I really do."

"I love you," Akoni said. "You know that."

"I love you too," Lakali replied.

"Come here," Akoni said and pulled Lakali to him.

He leaned down and gave her a long kiss.

"Lakali and Akoni forever," he said.

"Lakali and Akoni forever," she replied.

"I'd better go, but get some rest," Akoni reiterated.

"I will," Lakali replied. "Don't work too hard."

"I never do," Akoni grinned and headed out.

It wasn't true, though. Akoni was as much of a hard worker as anyone else on the island.

Lakali watched him leave. She felt bad that she was keeping a secret from him.

Again, making sure that the door was closed tightly, she went back to her trinket box. Feeling braver this time, seeing how nothing bad had happened to her the last time she opened it when she wasn't supposed to, she sat down in her chair and opened the box.

She studied the crystal for a long time. She looked at the colors hidden deep within it. What was it about the crystal that had such power over her? She remembered clearly what it felt like when the clear-thinking session began. Again, she could feel the urge it had on her when she finally gave in and came to gaze upon the crystal.

Seeing it like it was now, it was so hard to understand. Would she ever figure it out? She didn't know, but she knew she had to try.

In the meantime, she had to convince Akoni that everything was okay. The last thing she needed was for him to be worried about her and even be considering that he should go to the leaders for help. She decided that she would do her best to have a good evening with him. She would have him see how happy and rested she was so that he would no longer be worried about her.

She did need to get some rest. She wanted desperately to go back to bed and have that nap she had promised Akoni she would take. Would she have another bad dream? The thought of it was almost too much to bear. Still, she was exhausted. She really did need to lie down and rest if she was going to be able to give a convincing performance after dinner. She drifted off to sleep quickly.

"Catch me if you can!" Lakali shouted joyfully.

There were two other children with her.

"That's right. Go after her!" Caristiona yelled. "She's slower than I am. You'll catch her first!"

"I'm faster than both of you!" Akoni shouted back, but he had chosen his target.

He ran around the playground, chasing Lakali. Caristiona watched them and laughed.

Finally catching up to Lakali, Akoni could have quickly tagged her and moved on. Instead, he caught her and gave her a kiss on the cheek.

"You're it!" Akoni shouted and darted off.

Lakali blushed. Akoni had never kissed her before. They were just friends. She did think he was cute, though. At eleven years old, she was starting to pay more attention to boys. She was momentarily distracted from chasing him, thinking about the kiss he had planted on her cheek.

"Come on, Lakali. You're too slow!" Akoni teased her. "Catch me if you can!"

"You're mine!" Lakali shouted back, not realizing the true meaning of her words at the time.

Akoni was going to be hers for a long time to come.

The dream that Lakali was having was more than just some fantasy. It was a true memory, the memory of the first time Akoni had ever kissed her. Of course, neither of them had remembered it. The memory had faded from their minds after they were released from the playground.

Lakali woke up as the dream ended. Somehow, she knew in her heart that it was a true memory. It was such a nice one. To think that it had been stolen from her! Lakali couldn't help but feel a bit angry when she realized that it had been taken from her. She wondered how many other memories had been stolen as well. Still, she was at least grateful that it had been a good dream and not another nightmare.

She sighed and closed her eyes. What she really wanted was to go back to sleep and not have any more dreams at all. Fortunately, she didn't. When she awoke, Lakali found that sleeping an extra half hour really did help her feel better, if only a little. She went to work and helped the women finish dinner. She was relieved that all of the work requiring the use of a knife had already been done. The rest of the job would be pretty easy. She was assigned to watch the fish stew that was cooking over the fire.

Since Lakali had dinner duty, that meant she also had to help with cleanup. She only took a break to get something to eat. By the time she was done with work, Akoni had already eaten and was in the water going for a swim. Lakali went to her hut and put on her bathing suit. She went out to join him.

The sun was going down. But tonight, there was a full moon. It was still easy to see. Even so, Akoni had come closer to the shore, not wanting to be too far out in case there were any predators like sharks that wouldn't be easy to see at night. While they didn't usually come close to shore, it was always better to be safe than sorry.

Akoni saw Lakali coming to join him. He greeted her and pulled her to him, giving her a long gentle kiss. They were standing where the water came up to the top of Lakali's legs.

"Did you get Amzi's chair fixed?" Lakali asked.

"Yeah, we did," Akoni confirmed. "It wasn't that hard, and it helped when everyone decided to postpone most of the work on the boat until morning."

"In that case, I'm sorry I had to work so late," Lakali said. "We might have had some time to spend together. I hope you had a good swim."

"I did," Akoni replied. "It was good exercise."

"Do you want to go for a stroll on the beach?" Lakali asked.

"That sounds great," Akoni answered.

They walked closer to shore so that only their feet were in the water. They had their arms around each other's waists.

"I missed you at dinner," Akoni said. "I hate when you have to work the dinner shift."

"Me too," Lakali replied. "But someone has to prepare the food."

"You ladies outdid yourself tonight. That stew was delicious," Akoni complimented her.

"We couldn't have done it if it weren't for all our strong fishermen who bring us the fish," Lakali replied.

They stopped walking, and Akoni turned Lakali to face him. He reached down to kiss her again. They stood on the beach, kissing for several minutes.

"Do you want to go back to your hut?" Akoni asked.

He wanted privacy with Lakali. Even though no one was paying much mind to them, there were other islanders sitting outside their huts or relaxing on the beach. A few couples stood around doing exactly what Lakali and Akoni were doing, stealing some kisses on the moonlit beach.

"No," Lakali said.

The last thing she wanted was to be anywhere near her crystal.

"I just want to be right here with you right now," she said. "Kiss me again."

Akoni did as requested. They continued kissing, and neither of them wanted to stop. Finally, Lakali pulled herself away just a little.

"Do you remember the first time you kissed me?" Lakali asked as she looked up at Akoni.

"Of course," Akoni replied. "Who wouldn't?"

"Tell me about it," Lakali encouraged him.

"It was our first walk along this beach as a couple," Akoni continued. "In fact, I think it was right about here. Is that what made you think of it?"

"Maybe," Lakali answered. "Tell me more. What did you do?"

Akoni pulled Lakali a little closer.

"I pulled you to me, something like this," he said.

He had one hand around her waist. With the other, he tilted her face upwards.

"I told you how beautiful you looked in the moonlight," Akoni said. "Then, I did this."

Akoni leaned his head down and gently kissed Lakali. He now put both hands around her waist and drew her close to him. They stayed like that, kissing each other, for several more minutes.

When they pulled apart, Lakali carefully asked a question.

"And that was our *first* kiss?" she said.

"Of course," Akoni replied. "Don't you remember it?"

"Of course I remember. I remember it as if it was yesterday," Lakali answered.

Akoni sensed there was something more that she wasn't telling him.

"Lakali, is there something else you are wondering about?" he asked.

Lakali wanted to talk to him about the playground, but she couldn't bring the subject up. Not yet.

"No, nothing. It's just..." she replied.

"What? What is it?" Akoni questioned.

"It's just that Bakita wonders when you're going to put a ring on my finger," Lakali changed the subject.

"What a surprise!" Akoni replied. "She's always thinking about weddings and trying to see who's going to wed next."

"Is there something wrong with that?" Lakali asked, truly wanting to know what Akoni thought of the subject.

"No, of course not," Akoni said. "Wait a minute. Is that what this has all been about? Is that what's been bothering you? Are you upset that I haven't married you yet?"

It all made sense now.

"No, that's not it at all," Lakali replied. "It's just something Bakita brought up. That's all. I shouldn't have even mentioned it."

"I'm not afraid of marriage," Akoni said. "I suppose Bakita thinks that I am, but I'm not. I just thought that we were happy as we are, for now. It doesn't mean we won't get married later."

"I know, Akoni," Lakali said. "Really. It's okay. I was just repeating what she said."

"Hmmm," Akoni replied. "Are you sure? If you're upset about it, I would want you to tell me."

"I'm not. I promise," Lakali said. "Just kiss me."

"Lakali..." Akoni began.

"Akoni, kiss me. Now!" Lakali commanded.

Akoni did as she asked. They stood there for several minutes, kissing each other eagerly.

"Are you sure you don't want me to come with you to your hut?" Akoni asked. "You know I would never pressure you to do anything you aren't comfortable doing. I just like being alone with you and having you to myself."

"I know. I like that too, but I'm tired. It's been a long day. I think what I'd really like to do is to go to bed and try to get a good night's sleep," Lakali said.

Akoni wasn't so sure that Lakali was being honest. He thought maybe his theory was right and that Lakali was upset that he hadn't proposed to her yet. It wasn't like he didn't plan on it. He knew that he would be spending the rest of his life with her. He just hadn't been ready to make it official yet. But still, if he thought for a moment that he would lose her, he would drop to one knee and propose to her right now!

"Are you sure you're alright?" he asked. "Did the nap help?"

"Yeah, it did," Lakali answered truthfully. "It just wasn't long enough. That's why I figured I should turn in early tonight. Maybe by tomorrow, I'll be all rested up."

"Well, I do want you to get back to feeling like yourself again," Akoni replied. "Let me walk you to your hut."

"Okay," Lakali said.

Akoni saw her to her hut and gave her one more kiss goodnight. Lakali walked in and laid down on her cot. It was true. She needed to get some sleep. She needed her rest. It would take strength to be able to resist the power of the crystal tomorrow, but she was determined that, somehow, she was going to be able to do it!

Chapter 8

The next morning, Akoni came to check on Lakali before going to work. He had a few minutes before he needed to head out. Lakali was already awake. Caristiona was going to be coming over to spend the morning with her. Lakali answered the door right away when Akoni knocked. She invited him in, and they sat on her cot.

Akoni leaned over and kissed Lakali.

"Good morning," he said.

"Didn't you say that when you greeted me at the door?" Lakali questioned.

"So? I'm saying it again," Akoni replied. "It's always a good morning if I get to sneak in a few kisses before going to work."

"Mmmm," Lakali replied. "I see what you mean. Kiss me again."

Akoni had no problem doing as he was instructed.

"I can't get too caught up in this," he said. "Time gets away from me quickly when I'm with you."

"I wonder why that is," Lakali replied.

Akoni started to kiss her again, but Lakali stopped him. She needed to ask him about the playground, but she had to be careful. She didn't want him to think that anything was wrong.

"What?" Akoni asked. "Are you still upset about last night?"

"Last night?" Lakali questioned.

"Yes, our conversation about marriage and Bakita wanting me to put a ring on your finger," Akoni answered.

"No, of course not," Lakali replied. "And I wasn't upset last night. I told you that."

"Then, what is it?" Akoni asked.

"It's nothing bad," Lakali replied. "It's just something I was wondering."

"What?" Akoni inquired.

"It's just that I was wondering about the clear-thinking sessions," Lakali continued. "I was wondering about the children. What do they do while we have our sessions?"

Akoni thought about it for a moment.

"I suppose they wait for the adults," he finally replied.

He honestly didn't know what they did.

"Is that what we did?" Lakali asked.

"I don't know," Akoni replied honestly. "I suppose it was."

"But you don't remember?" Lakali asked.

"No. Do you?" Akoni questioned.

"No, I don't remember either," Lakali lied.

So, Akoni had no recollection of the playground. It was what Lakali had expected. Still, a part of her was disappointed. She wanted him to remember their happy time there together and their first kiss. It was true that it wasn't anything like their first kiss on the beach. Still, it was a nice memory. Lakali wanted to hang onto it. She also worried about why she was the only one who could remember the playground.

"It's because we were so young," Akoni replied. "It's hard to remember things from when you're that young."

"I suppose," Lakali said, but her voice sounded distant.

"You don't think that's why?" Akoni inquired.

"I don't know," Lakali replied. "I mean, I can remember other things from my childhood. Why can't I remember what I was doing during the sessions?"

Akoni thought about it for a minute.

"I don't know," he finally replied. "I guess it would make sense that we should remember something, but we don't. Surely, this is a question that our leaders could answer."

"It's a silly question," Lakali replied. "The leaders are much too busy to be bothered with such a minor thing."

"I suppose you're right," Akoni agreed. "Still, it's going to make me wonder now. Perhaps we should ask a child what they do when we have our sessions. Surely, they could remember. They are still young, after all."

"I don't think that would be a good idea," Lakali replied honestly.

"Why not?" Akoni asked.

"I just think it would make us look like we're questioning things, like we're questioning our leaders' judgment," Lakali answered. "And of course, neither of us would do that."

"We aren't questioning it," Akoni replied. "We're just curious."

"Anything regarding the clear-thinking sessions could be looked upon as if we were questioning them," Lakali insisted. "It's best if we keep these questions between us. Promise me."

"I suppose you're right, and I promise," Akoni said. "It's not important anyway. You just got my curiosity up. That's all."

"I know, and I'm sorry," Lakali replied. "My mind wanders too much."

"Yes, it does," Akoni agreed. "You have seriously got to stop thinking all the time. Live for the moment. That's what I do."

"That's what you do?" Lakali questioned.

"All the time," Akoni smiled and leaned over to give Lakali a long, soft kiss.

"That's my Akoni," Lakali said. "Always wanting to kiss me."

"I've never known you to have any objections," Akoni replied.

"Oh, I never said I objected," Lakali said and pulled Akoni closer to her for another kiss.

Akoni kissed her back and then reluctantly pulled away.

"I told you I can't get this distracted today," he said.

"It's never fair," Lakali replied.

"No, it's never fair," Akoni agreed. "But I have to go now. I'll be thinking about your kisses the whole time I'm at work."

"You'd better be," Lakali said.

They had one more brief kiss. Then, Akoni stood up to leave. All he wanted was to stay with Lakali, but he had responsibilities.

When he got to the door, he blew her another kiss. Lakali pretended to catch it and then held her hands to her heart.

"I love you," Akoni said.

"I love you more," Lakali replied.

Akoni went back to work, and Lakali was left to her thoughts.

"It's true," she thought to herself. "It's not fair. It's not fair that I can remember our time in the playground and Akoni can't. It's not fair that I can't tell anyone about my horrible daymares. It's not fair that I'm afraid to go to the leaders. It's not fair, not fair at all."

Chapter 9

Caristiona came over a couple of minutes after Akoni left. Lakali greeted her, happy to see her friend and happy for a distraction from her thoughts.

"It doesn't matter how early I get here. That boy always gets to you first," Caristiona said.

"I can't help it if he's head-over-heels in love with me, can I?" Lakali asked.

"No, but you can tell him that you need to spend more time with me," Caristiona replied.

"What? Like it's any different with you? I'm surprised you could get a morning away from Amzi," Lakali said. "That poor husband of yours is lost without you."

"Good for me he had to go help in the fishing boats this morning, isn't it?" Caristiona replied.

"Yes, I suppose so," Lakali answered. "I'm surprised they let him back on the fishing boats after what happened last time!"

No one stayed in one job for very long. The islanders rotated tasks. It was the leaders' wise decision that they do so. It ensured that no one got too bored or discouraged if they had to do a job they didn't like. It also made things more fair so that no islander got stuck in a job that required constant strenuous physical exertion.

Caristiona shuddered at the memory that Lakali had brought up. Admittedly, fishermen always came home stinking of fish. But that day, Amzi had tripped while on the boat and had fallen face-down into a huge pile of fish that was piled up in the center of the boat. Fish had been strewn everywhere, and the others had to help pull Amzi out of the pile and get all the fish back to the center of the boat. Of course, they had laughed severely at Amzi and hadn't let him live it down. His clothes were hopeless. Caristiona had been forced to burn them.

"He promised me he is hanging by the deck and doing no more than passing the fish on to the other fishermen to place in the pile," Caristiona said. "I told him if he comes back smelling like that again, he'd better not be coming back at all!"

"Oh, you did not," Lakali replied. "You would never turn him away. Besides, what about little Amzi?"

Lakali patted Caristiona's belly.

"I did say it," Caristiona insisted. "But of course, Amzi knew I was teasing him. And why do you say little Amzi? I'm thinking it's little Cari!"

Caristiona smiled.

"We can't have too many men in our family, now can we?" she asked.

Caristiona came from a large family. She had five brothers and only one sister. She believed it was only fair for her to have a girl, seeing how outnumbered the females were in her family.

"You know you will love your child the same whether it's an Amzi or a Cari," Lakali stated.

"That's true," Caristiona said. "But I do hope it's a girl. It would be so nice!"

Caristiona was only about three months along in her pregnancy and was barely showing. The small bulge on her tummy could easily be mistaken for a little added weight. Only those close to her knew she was expecting a child. Others teased her to lay off the pastries, telling her that Amzi might have to go looking elsewhere if she kept gaining weight. Of course, Amzi would never look elsewhere.

He was as hopelessly in love with Caristiona as she was with him.

Lakali and Caristiona spent the morning going for a walk along the beach barefoot. Both of them loved the feel of the sand under their feet. They walked close to the water, letting it slosh over their feet as they strolled along. They shared stories of what had been happening in their lives. A week had passed since the last time they were able to relax and enjoy each other's company like this. Between their work schedules and being with their men, it seemed like it was getting harder to find much time to spend together. Of course, Lakali didn't tell Caristiona anything about her daymares.

They came close to where the fishing boats docked. They stopped and looked out to the ocean. Caristiona put her hand over her eyes to shield them from the sun and squinted. She thought she could see Amzi's boat as she looked out toward the horizon. The boat had gone about two miles out from the shore. It looked so small on the distant water.

"Do you think he's fallen face-first yet?" Lakali teased. "I'll bet he's rolling in the fish right about now."

"He is not," Caristiona answered. "He wouldn't dare!"

The girls laughed and turned to head back the way they had come.

"Where is Akoni today?" Caristiona asked.

"He's helping rebuild a hut that is falling apart over in Section Seven," Lakali answered.

"I heard that there were several huts over there needing repairs," Caristiona replied. "Most of the huts there have never been rebuilt, or at least, that's what I was told. I suppose it's past time. I'm sure they're really old by now."

"Yeah, I suppose so," Lakali replied. "I suspect Akoni will be working over there for a while."

The islanders were divided up into small neighborhoods called sections. It was a large island. There were fifteen sections in all. Disbursing the islanders like this kept them from feeling too crowded, and there was plenty of land and nature around the sections so that the island remained peaceful. Lakali and Caristiona lived in Section Five.

The women returned to Caristiona's hut and sat in the sun, chatting. The fishing boats would be back within a couple of hours. They had a rule that they must be back at least four hours before sunset because no one ever knew exactly when the clear-thinking sessions would begin. The leaders wanted every islander to benefit from them. The boats could only return to the water after the session ended. If it was too late in the day, that usually didn't happen.

While the two girls sat and talked, they discussed possible names for the baby. Lakali insisted that the child should have his or her own name and not just some variation of their parents' names.

"It would be too confusing," Lakali said. "Imagine if Amzi is calling you and you hear your name, only he's calling your daughter. You won't know who he wants."

"I never thought of it like that," Caristiona said. "But the name could be close, couldn't it?"

"I don't see why not," Lakali answered.

"Then, how about Carisola?" Caristiona asked.

"But you would both have the nickname Cari," Lakali reminded her.

"We wouldn't have to," Caristiona insisted. "We could call her Sola."

"Sola?" Lakali asked.

"Yeah, what's wrong with that?" Caristiona asked.

"I don't know," Lakali replied. "I've just never heard that name before, but I guess it would work."

"Good. Then Carisola it is!" her friend proclaimed.

"*If* it's a girl," Lakali reminded her.

"You worry too much," Caristiona said. "It will definitely be a girl. Just wait and see!"

They began to reminisce about their youth and the adventures they had together playing in the ocean and climbing the hills, and of course, flirting with boys.

"You always had a crush on Akoni," Caristiona said. "I could see it even if you wouldn't admit it!"

"How did you know?" Lakali asked.

"You couldn't take your eyes off of him," Caristiona replied. "It was awkward really, you constantly averting your eyes whenever he looked your way. But I guess it worked for you."

She hadn't averted her eyes that day on the playground. Did Caristiona remember that day also? Most likely, she had no recollection of it. Lakali decided it was best not to ask her about it.

"Eventually," Lakali said. "It took me long enough to get him!"

"He was just shy," Caristiona replied. "You both were. It's a wonder he ever got the nerve to ask you out."

Akoni hadn't seemed shy on the playground. Now that Lakali thought of it, it was almost as if their personalities had changed while they were there. Was it the peacefulness that they had felt? Did that relax them and give them the courage to act more boldly than they normally could?

"That boy always loved you," Caristiona continued.

"Speaking of..." Lakali said as she saw Akoni approaching them.

"Hey you!" Caristiona yelled, and Akoni looked to see that Lakali was sitting with her. "When are you putting a ring on my friend's finger?!"

"Stop!" Lakali tried to quiet Caristiona without letting Akoni hear her.

Akoni now stood in front of them.

"I can see you two ladies are working hard today, or should I say hardly working?" Akoni teased.

"It's our day off," Caristiona replied. "Besides, I'm an expectant mother. I'm allowed to take it easy, aren't I?"

"I won't argue with you there or I'm sure I'd get my ear chewed off!" Akoni answered.

"You're avoiding my question," Caristiona said.

"Shut up," Lakali tried to quiet her.

"When are you marrying my friend?" Caristiona asked. "Everyone is talking about it and wondering when the wedding will be."

"Who said there *was* going to be a wedding?" Akoni replied, not because he didn't want to marry Lakali as that was what he wanted most but because he wanted to give Caristiona a hard time.

"Hey! That wasn't nice!" Caristiona said. "Just for that, Lakali is not going to allow you to touch her again until you offer her a ring."

Akoni looked at Lakali and raised his eyebrow.

"Is that true?" he asked.

"It might be," Lakali said uncertainly.

"Look! Here comes Amzi!" Caristiona stood up and changed the subject.

The fishing boats were back. Sure enough, her husband was approaching.

"Do you smell like fish?" Caristiona called.

"I've been fishing! What do you expect?" Amzi called back.

"You'd best not be coming in to see me until you go bathe!" Caristiona yelled.

"I was going to come scoop you up and hold you close and give you a big slobbery kiss!" Amzi yelled.

"Oh, no you don't!" Caristiona shouted, but she could see that Amzi was starting to run her way.

"Here I come!" Amzi shouted as he came running toward the hut.

Caristiona jumped up and headed for the water, figuring if he was going to catch her with those smelly clothes on, they should at least be in the water.

Lakali and Akoni watched them and laughed. Then, Akoni drew his attention back to Lakali.

"So, what's the verdict?" he asked. "Am I allowed to touch you?"

Lakali felt awkward, not knowing what to say. Of course she wanted him to touch her, but she wondered if he had been serious. Did he really *not* want to ever marry her? Had the truth just slipped out?

She opened her mouth to reply, but she didn't get a word out before the feeling came over her. The intense desire and need to return to her hut and to go to her trinket box... Akoni felt it also. He turned from Lakali and started to walk away from her. At the beach, Amzi and Caristiona separated and walked as if in a trance toward their hut. They didn't say anything but walked in silence.

Without even thinking about it, Lakali fell in line with the other islanders, her eyes pointed toward her own hut about fifty yards away. She walked with a great urgency, her trinket box calling to her.

"Don't look at the crystal," Lakali muttered to herself over and over as she headed toward the hut.

Even though her eyes were locked on her hut, she was now more aware than ever of what was happening. She could see the islanders walking helplessly back to their huts, unable to control any of their actions, completely under the power of their own trinket boxes. Lakali got to her hut and opened the door. She went to the trinket box and picked it up. She sat down on the mat. Her eyes immediately fell to the box. No! She couldn't look. She had to be strong, but she wanted to look at the crystal so badly!

Lakali took a deep breath and let it out slowly. Something told her that it was critical to *not* look inside that box when she opened it. She tried to stop her hand from opening the box, but it was a programmed response. She had no control over what she was doing as her right hand touched the lid and began to open it. It took all of Lakali's mental strength, but she averted her eyes and fixed them on the door of her hut.

It was as if a great presence was in the room with her, demanding her to look. She could see the light of the crystal shining in a cone around her. It called to her. She could see traces of green and pink and lavender and silver flash around the room, beckoning her to just take a quick peek. But Lakali stayed strong and didn't take her eyes off the door.

Now that she was resisting the power of the crystal, she was alert and awake to the things that were happening around her. In what was mostly silence, she could hear a faint hum coming from the crystal inside the trinket box. She strained her ears to hear what was happening outside and could hear approaching footsteps as they shuffled through the sand. She could barely hear the sound of someone breathing and whispering, or was that just the wind?

As she stared at the door, she saw the knob start to turn. Lakali panicked and looked away, almost locking eyes on the crystal. She was looking just above the trinket box, her eyes within an inch of staring at the frightening object. Lakali made a huge discovery in that brief moment. If she could avert her eyes to look just above the trinket box, it would appear as if she was staring at the crystal. Yet that short distance allowed her to remain awake. She wasn't under the power of the crystal.

The door opened. From the corner of her eye, Lakali noticed that the person looking in at her was one of their leaders. He looked to Lakali on the mat, supposedly transfixed by the crystal. Satisfied she was under its power, he closed the door and moved on. Lakali could hear him say something softly.

"Section Five secured," he said.

Lakali focused on her breathing. In and out, in and out... She had to think about what she was doing. The power of the crystal still called to her, and it still felt like there was a strong commanding presence in the room with her. She refused to give in to it. She willed herself to stay awake and alert. The more she willed it, the easier it seemed. While she still had to conscientiously think about what she was doing to keep herself awake, she felt stronger than she had ever been. She knew that she could beat the crystal and not succumb to its hold that it wanted to put on her.

She didn't know how much time was passing, but she estimated that it was close to an hour before the crystal's light went out and she no longer felt the desire to look at it. She let out her breath. She had survived it. No daymare had plagued her. She finally looked down at the crystal. It looked so harmless, sitting in the box like that. She closed the lid, got up and placed the box on the shelf. She began to have second thoughts. Was it a good thing that she had missed out on the clear-thinking session? The leaders surely would know what was best for the islanders. They had been in charge for as long as anyone could remember. Would something bad happen to her now that she had missed out on one of her sessions?

And yet, it was as if she was now thinking more clearly than ever. She couldn't explain it. Her head felt much clearer than it had ever felt, and she believed that she had done the right thing. She didn't understand any of it. What was it about the crystal that scared her so much? Was it just the daymares? They would truly be enough to frighten anyone, but Lakali could sense that there was something deeper and more distressful about the crystal that was bothering her.

Lakali wanted to go see Caristiona. Their time together had been interrupted by the clear-thinking session. As she exited her hut, Akoni met her and saw she was headed somewhere.

"Where are you going?" he asked.

"To see Caristiona," Lakali replied.

"Didn't you have enough time with her this morning?" Akoni asked.

"Maybe not," Lakali said. "Don't you need to return to work?"

"We finished the hut this morning," Akoni said. "It wasn't as bad as we expected. I thought we could spend the afternoon together."

"You need to get cleaned up," Lakali said. "I'll see you later."

Lakali kept walking, paying no more attention to Akoni. She was still irritated by his comment about not marrying her. Akoni couldn't even remember the last few minutes before the clear-thinking session and didn't know why she was upset with him.

"Did I do something?" he called after her.

"You know what you did," Lakali answered and kept heading forward, not even stopping to look back at Akoni as she answered him.

Akoni was baffled. There was no figuring out women sometimes. He would have to talk to her later and try to find out what was bothering her. Lakali was right about one thing. He did need to clean up. He shrugged off Lakali's behavior and headed out to bathe.

Lakali got to Caristiona's hut and knocked on the door. Caristiona greeted her and smiled.

"Come on in," Caristiona said. "I was just looking at some drawings I made when I was younger. Do you remember this one?"

Caristiona was very talented and could draw anyone and make them look almost as perfect as they were in real life. She handed Lakali a picture she had drawn of Akoni. Even in the picture, Akoni was so handsome that Lakali felt a tinge of regret at how she had just treated him.

"It's very lifelike," Lakali said. "You should show it to him."

As they looked through the drawings, Lakali found one that Caristiona had drawn of Amzi.

"He's very handsome also," Lakali mentioned.

Caristiona looked at the picture and seemed confused.

"Yes, he is," she replied. "I just wish I knew who he was. I wouldn't mind meeting him!"

Lakali laughed.

"You're such a jokester," she said.

"What do you mean?" Caristiona asked and looked at Lakali with true confusion in her eyes.

"What?" Lakali asked.

Now, it was her turn to be confused.

"You can't be serious?" she asked. "What do you mean, you don't know who he is?"

"I don't," Caristiona assured her. "I don't recall ever seeing him before. But like you said, he is quite handsome. I suppose I must have drawn this years ago and forgot about him, whoever he is."

Lakali was confused. She looked around. Where was Amzi? Had he left to clean up?

"Where's Amzi?" she asked aloud.

"Who?" Caristiona asked.

"Amzi!" Lakali now shouted. "Your husband!"

Caristiona burst out laughing.

"Oh, now *you're* the jokester!" she said. "Husband? I don't have a husband, silly!"

"If you don't have a husband, why are you wearing a wedding ring?" Lakali asked.

But as she looked down at Caristiona's hand, she was horrified to see that her friend's wedding ring was missing.

"What?" Lakali asked. "Where's your ring?"

Now, Caristiona looked worried. There was something wrong with her friend.

"Are you feeling alright?" she asked Lakali. "Did you not have a good clear-thinking session?"

"What? No! It's not me!" Lakali practically shouted. "This is crazy! Amzi was here an hour ago! He has to be here somewhere!"

Lakali began walking around, looking for any evidence that might link Amzi to the hut. She needed something to prove to Caristiona that Amzi existed and was her husband, but she couldn't find anything.

Caristiona was becoming scared. She had no idea what was making her friend act this way.

"Okay, then," Lakali finally said. "If you're not married, then who is the father of the child you are carrying?!"

Caristiona laughed again, but this time it was more of a frightened laugh than one of true humor.

"That isn't even funny," Caristiona answered. "I'm *not* pregnant."

"Of course you are," Lakali replied. "You need to remember."

"I've just gained a little weight," Caristiona insisted. "It's rather rude for you to accuse me of becoming pregnant while I am still unmarried.

"But you *are* married!" Lakali shouted. "You have a husband. Amzi, the man in that portrait! Please! Try to remember!"

"You need to see the leaders," Caristiona said. "You're not well."

Lakali's head was spinning. Something was terribly wrong. Her friend had no memory of her own husband, and Lakali had a sinking feeling that Amzi wasn't coming back. Whatever had happened to him had erased his very existence from Caristiona's memory.

Lakali panicked. She remembered the leader checking her hut and saying the section was cleared. Something wasn't right, and she was beginning to think that whatever sinister thing was happening to the islanders had to do with their leaders. She knew she couldn't let them find out that she was awake and was asking about Amzi.

"I'm sorry," she said. "You're right. My session just didn't go well. That must be it. It put false memories in my mind."

"Then, the leaders need to know for sure," Caristiona insisted. "They would want to know so they could fix it. I should go and speak to them for you."

"No!" Lakali shouted. "Please, don't! I'm just tired. I'll go home and take a nap. I'll feel much better later. I promise!"

"Are you sure?" Caristiona asked. "I don't mind going to them on your behalf."

"Please promise me you won't," Lakali begged.

"Okay, fine," Caristiona said. "But if tomorrow's session goes like this, I won't take no for an answer. I will go to get you some help. You are my friend, after all."

"I promise. Tomorrow's session will be great!" Lakali tried to assure her friend.

"Very well," Caristiona said. "Go home and take a nap so that I won't worry so much about you."

"I will," Lakali promised.

She hugged her friend and left the hut, hoping that Caristiona would keep her word and not tell the leaders about what had happened. She knew that she had to keep her eyes open, but that she had to be careful what she said in the future. She couldn't let Caristiona see that she was questioning things. She must convince her tomorrow that her session went well. She made a promise to herself to come see her tomorrow, just to show Caristiona that she was fine so that she wouldn't feel any need to report her to the leaders.

Lakali couldn't believe that Caristiona had forgotten Amzi. Where was he anyway? And what about the baby? Her friend was pregnant, whether she believed it or not. When her baby was born, the child wouldn't know anything about Amzi, not if he didn't show up again. Lakali suspected that wasn't going to happen, though. He was gone forever, and his whole family would forget all about him.

A sudden thought came to Lakali. Had she forgotten anyone like Caristiona had forgotten Amzi? Had there been people in her own life who were now gone forever? And what about her parents? Was what she had been told about them even true? No, she couldn't let herself think about that right now.

It was all so confusing and upsetting. Lakali wanted to escape from it all, but she knew that there would be no rest for her weary spirit. Now, on top of the memory of the horrible daymares, she would constantly wonder who she had forgotten about and would have questions that she doubted she would ever get answers to.

That evening, the islanders were having a gathering. They were roasting pig over a large fire while some of the more talented islanders were dancing and singing. Some of them carried torches blazing with fire. They threw the lit torches above them, juggling them and catching them while they danced on a small platform constructed by some of the men in Section Three. The islanders from four other sections had come to join them, and it was a large gathering. There were similar celebrations occurring throughout the island. It was the landmark anniversary of the day when their ancestors had first discovered the island so long ago.

Of course, no one really knew much about their history. Very little information had been handed down to them over the years. Aside from the stories that Lakali remembered about how the island had called to its new inhabitants who had been fleeing some war, no one really knew much more. Still, the leaders thought it was important that this significant date be remembered and celebrated. For the leaders, their whole lives revolved around this history. Without the islanders who had come to live here, the island wouldn't be much of a home for anyone.

Lakali and Akoni found a secluded area among the palm trees. They sat on the ground leaning against a large palm and nestled close to each other. Lakali leaned her head back against Akoni's shoulder. Akoni kissed her on the forehead.

"You still haven't told me why you were upset with me earlier," Akoni said.

"It was nothing, really," Lakali answered, knowing she couldn't explain to Akoni how she remembered something that he didn't recall even saying.

"You said I had done something," Akoni reminded her. "It would be nice to know so that I don't do it again. I don't like it when you're upset with me."

"Really, it's nothing," Lakali insisted. "I'd like to forget it. Please, can we just enjoy the show?"

"Sure," Akoni said. "Just don't say that I didn't try to fix things."

"Things are fixed already," Lakali assured him.

"Do you want some more food?" Akoni asked. "I'd be glad to go get you some."

"I'm stuffed," Lakali answered. "I couldn't eat another bite, but something to drink might be nice."

"At your service!" Akoni said and gently moved Lakali aside so that he could go get her a cup of coconut milk.

When Akoni left, Caristiona saw her chance to go check on her friend. She came and sat down by Lakali.

"How are you feeling?" she asked.

"I'm fine. Really," Lakali lied.

"You gave me such a scare today speaking gibberish and all," Caristiona said.

"I know," Lakali replied. "I was just seriously sleep-deprived. I've had insomnia the last few nights."

"Sleep deprivation will mess with your head, but I've never seen it that severe before," Caristiona said. "You do look tired. You'd better get some sleep tonight. No late night with Akoni!"

"Sure," Lakali said. "Anything you say."

"Hmmm," Caristiona replied. "You sure agreed to that quickly. Are you sure that things are alright between you and Akoni? You seemed rather put out with him earlier today."

"We're fine," Lakali answered.

"Is it because he can't make a commitment?" Caristiona asked.

"Who says he can't make a commitment?" Lakali inquired.

"Is there a ring on your finger?" Caristiona asked.

"There will be," Lakali replied. "In time."

"Well, I say there has been enough time," Caristiona said. "That boy is wasting your time and dragging his feet!"

"You nag too much," Lakali replied.

She almost asked if Caristiona nagged at Amzi too much, but then she remembered that her friend had no recollection of being married. Lakali stopped herself just in time.

"Sometimes you need to nag," Caristiona replied. "Sometimes it is the only way to get others to do the right thing. Someday when I am married, I will nag my husband as much as I need to if that's what he needs."

"I'm sure you will," Lakali said. "It's a good thing you have a good heart."

"Good indeed!" Caristiona responded.

"So, what are you two ladies discussing?"

Akoni asked as he brought Lakali a small cup of coconut milk.

"You!" Caristiona answered.

"Uh-oh," Akoni said.

"That's right," Caristiona replied. "You'd better be worried, and you'd better keep worrying all the time until you're ready to put a ring on her finger!"

"Is that all you ever think of?" Akoni asked.

"Of course," Caristiona answered. "You men always want to avoid marriage for as long as possible. It's the job of us women to make you settle down!'

"Yeah? Well, if you're so good at your job, how come you don't have a husband yet?" Akoni asked.

"I'm working on it!" Caristiona replied. "I just have to find the right man!"

"It sounds like you're the one who can't make a commitment!" Akoni accused her.

He smiled, showing that he wasn't really angry. He enjoyed these arguments that Caristiona liked to engage in.

"Well!" Caristiona said and pretended to be upset. "This conversation is getting us nowhere quick! I will leave you two lovebirds alone. Not that it will do any good. I doubt that I will see a ring on Lakali's finger by morning. But if she's wise, she won't allow you too many kisses until you do the right thing!"

Akoni sat down and put his arm around Lakali.

"Hmmm," he said. "What do you think about that? How many kisses should I be allowed to steal?"

He started to lean down to kiss Lakali, but her mind was racing. She moved away and stood up to stretch. Akoni looked up at her, wondering what was wrong.

"Have I done something again?" he asked.

Lakali didn't answer him. She was too deep in thought. So, Akoni had no memory of Caristiona being married either. She didn't understand what was happening. Was she going crazy? No! She knew that Amzi had existed and had disappeared, and she knew it had something to do with the crystals and the clear-thinking session. But she couldn't tell anyone. No one would believe her.

Akoni stood up and came to stand behind Lakali. He put his hands against her waist and pulled her backward until her body was leaning into his.

"Did I do something wrong?" he repeated.

"Do you know a man named Amzi?" Lakali asked, needing to know what he would say.

"Amzi?" Akoni asked. "I can't say that I do, but the name does sound vaguely familiar."

Lakali turned, excited now, thinking that maybe Akoni could remember Amzi if she just pushed him hard enough.

"Think!" she said. "Try to remember him, for me!"

Akoni tried to search his mind. He knew he had heard the name before, but he couldn't place where he had heard it.

"I can't remember," he said. "I mean, I know I've heard of him, but it must be an old memory because I can't place him."

"Oh, Akoni, try harder! Please!" Lakali begged.

"Why is this so important?" Akoni asked.

"It just is," Lakali answered. "You need to trust me on this. I *need* you to remember him."

"Well, I can't," Akoni replied. "I don't know what to tell you. You look beautiful, though. To be honest, right now, I don't care who he is. It's you who I want to think about."

He leaned down to kiss her, but Lakali pushed him away.

"What?!" Akoni asked loudly, sincerely frustrated with Lakali now.

"I told you," Lakali said. "I need you to try to remember Amzi! All you ever want to do is kiss. There are other things in life that are important also!"

"Oh, now I get it," Akoni replied. "The truth is you don't want to be here with me. You want to be with this Amzi guy! Is this your way of breaking up with me?!"

"What?! No!" Lakali replied. "It's not that at all!"

"Well then, who is this Amzi that you want me to remember so badly?" Akoni asked. "I think you owe me an explanation!"

"If I tell you, you won't believe me," Lakali said.

"Oh, yeah? Try me!" Akoni insisted.

Lakali let out a sigh. She didn't know what to do. Could she nudge his memory if she told him who Amzi was? She didn't know what else to do, so she decided to give it a try.

"Amzi is Caristiona's husband," Lakali said.

Akoni burst out laughing.

"What?!" he finally asked. "What did she do? Secretly marry or something?"

"No, it was a very public wedding," Lakali answered. "You and I attended the wedding together. I caught the bridal bouquet. Why can't you remember?"

Akoni looked at Lakali like she was crazy.

"Is this a joke or what?" he asked.

"I'm not joking!" she said.

Then, lowering her voice to a whisper, she

leaned in toward Akoni.

"Something weird is happening, and I need you to trust me," she said. "I'm telling you that Caristiona has a husband, and he's gone missing. Now, she can't even remember him, and neither can you!"

"But *you* can?" Akoni asked. "You can remember this so-called husband, but his own wife cannot remember him, or anyone else, for that matter? And I'm supposed to believe that there is something wrong? Well, there obviously *is* something wrong, but it is something wrong with you. Do you not feel well? Perhaps you should go see the leaders. They would be able to figure out what is wrong with you."

"No!" Lakali said. "I can't go to the leaders! They're behind whatever is happening."

"Lakali," Akoni said with concern in his voice. "You sound crazy. I'm worried about you. Let me help. Let the leaders help. I can't watch you fall apart like this."

Lakali backed a few feet away from Akoni.

"You're going to turn me in, aren't you?!" she asked.

"I want to help," Akoni replied.

"You'll get me killed!" Lakali said.

"I would never..." Akoni responded.

"You don't know what you will do!" Lakali replied. "You cannot speak to the leaders! Promise me! If you speak to them, I promise you that I will never speak to you again!"

"Lakali! Be reasonable!" Akoni begged.

"No! I mean it! If you speak to them, you will lose me forever!" Lakali said. "You will have to make that decision!"

"Fine," Akoni agreed. "I won't speak to them, not now anyway. But you must promise me to stop talking about all of this nonsense."

"Fine," Lakali said. "I won't talk about it anymore. Just don't go to the leaders. Please! If you ever cared anything about me, keep your word!"

"Care anything about you?" Akoni replied. "Lakali, I love you! Don't you know that?!"

"I guess," Lakali answered. "You just have to keep your word. You just have to!"

Akoni approached Lakali and drew her to him. He held her tightly and she rested her face on his chest.

"I promise," he said. "This conversation never even took place as far as I'm concerned. Just please don't be upset with me."

"Okay," Lakali replied. "Just hold me and don't ever let go!"

"I won't," Akoni said. "You're my girl forever. I'll put a ring on your finger if that's what you need from me."

Lakali looked up.

"You would do that for me?" she asked.

"Of course," Akoni replied. "I've known for some time that you would eventually be my wife. I just wasn't rushing things."

"Oh, Akoni!" Lakali said and leaned her face back down on Akoni's chest.

She didn't know what she was going to do about the situation with Amzi, but she knew she couldn't discuss it with Akoni anymore. He couldn't remember Amzi anymore than Caristiona could, and Lakali knew that she was making herself look crazy talking like this. And what about Akoni's parents? He never spoke of them. Surely, he didn't remember them either. Could she make him understand that something was wrong if she asked him about them? She had made him question why he couldn't remember what happened to him during the clear-thinking sessions when he was a child. Perhaps if he thought about it, he would think it was odd that he couldn't remember his parents. Something must have happened to them. If something could have happened to them, perhaps what she was telling him about this Amzi person was true also.

But no, it was too dangerous. She had barely convinced him to not go to the leaders. She didn't dare bring anything else up now. She needed evidence and more information about what was happening during the clear-thinking sessions. She resolved herself to learn more and find out what was going on. For now, she would keep her worries to herself. When she had enough evidence, then she would approach Akoni and enlist his help. For now, she just wanted to live in the moment, feeling safe and loved by Akoni.

Chapter 10

The next afternoon, the fishing boats had once again barely returned when the islanders all went into a trance and started heading for their huts. Lakali followed along and pretended to be walking mindlessly to her hut as well. She still wondered how she was awake when the others were completely unaware of what they were doing. Lakali could only figure that it must have to do with the fact that she was aware of the power that the crystals had over her and all of the other islanders. Perhaps just knowing this had strengthened her mind and allowed her to resist the call of the crystal.

Today, it wasn't as hard for her. She still felt the need to go to her hut, but she felt confident and knew that she could resist the temptation to look at the crystal. She got to her hut, removed the box from the shelf, sat down on her mat and hesitated. She knew that as soon as she opened the box, the urge to look at the crystal would increase. She took several deep breaths, releasing them slowly until she felt she was strong enough to do what had to be done.

Lakali opened the box and averted her eyes immediately to the wall in front of her. She waited for the footsteps. They were quieter today, and there was no whispering to go along with them. She hardly knew the leader was even there until she heard his hand on her door. Quickly, she looked down, almost too fast, almost to the crystal itself. She blinked her eyes and focused them just over the rim of the box.

The leader looked in and saw Lakali on the

mat. For a moment, he wasn't sure she was really under the crystal's power. She didn't look as spellbound as the other islanders. He had noticed it yesterday too, but he had dismissed it. He walked into the hut and went to stand behind Lakali.

Lakali was frightened. She didn't know why the leader had come into her hut. Had Caristiona or Akoni turned her in? She fought to stay calm and not let herself think about her fears. She focused on her breathing. She must keep it steady and at a calm rate. She mustn't let the leader see that she was afraid or that she even felt his presence.

The leader reached down and gently lifted a handful of Lakali's dark hair. Lakali's mind was racing, but her body remained still as she focused on one thing. Breathe in, breathe out, breathe in, breathe out... The leader leaned down and sniffed Lakali's hair. It smelled good, filled with coconut. In fact, the girl herself smelled heavenly. He wondered... Should she be the one?

He was about to communicate with the others and tell them he had found a subject, but then he remembered that wasn't what today's session was about. Today was more important than acquiring a single subject. Today was the day when they would secure their future far beyond the needs of the day.

The leader made a mental note to not let too many days go by before acquiring this subject.

"Too bad," he whispered. "I would have enjoyed taking you to my friends."

With that, he turned and left, now fully convinced that Lakali was as transfixed and under the crystal's power as anyone else on the island.

After he left and closed the door behind him, Lakali started to cry. She could feel the tears slipping down her face as her whole body shook. She put the box on the mat and sat there, wrapping herself tightly in her arms and rocking back and forth as she cried quietly. Finally, after a couple of minutes, she knew that she had to be brave. She had to peek outside her hut, and she had to follow the leader and see where he was going.

Lakali carefully crept to the door and opened it only an inch. Seeing the coast was clear, she opened the door wider and peeked her head out. She could see the leader walking further up the shore, away from Caristiona's hut.

Lakali quickly and quietly left her hut. She followed at a distance, making sure to keep enough space between herself and the leader to allow herself to duck behind a hut or a tree if the leader thought to glance back. Whatever happened, Lakali knew it was critical that she not allow the leader to see her. Whatever it was that he had originally planned for her, she knew that if he spotted her, her fate would be even worse.

She continued to follow him until he got to the edge of her section. He continued walking, only much faster now. The speed with which he walked amazed Lakali. She knew she had to keep up, but how? She got to a point where there was a large hill to her left. She ran to it and climbed up, trying to get a better view. She could barely see the leader now, but it looked like he was heading north to the beach above Section Six. It was a small section. Its huts were the furthest from the beach of any section on the island. There were currently no islanders living in this section. Their numbers had dwindled. When they had gotten too low, they had been relocated to other sections. Their leaders explained to them that they needed to have more people with them to help with their daily work.

Lakali ran down the hill and hurried to get to Section Six. Going at a good speed, it would take her about ten more minutes to get there. The leader had traversed the distance in almost no time at all.

That alone frightened Lakali. How anyone could move that fast scared her. It was abnormal, but she couldn't think about that now. She had to know what he was up to.

Even though Lakali was hurrying, she also took care to move quietly and to stay where there was plenty of cover to not be seen. After another ten minutes of running, she finally came to the edge of Section Six. She could see the island's leaders standing together on the beach discussing something important.

Taking a moment to catch her breath as she hid behind a hut and making sure that she wasn't too close for them to hear her, Lakali took in the air around her and relished it as the oxygen filled her lungs. She hadn't run that much in years and knew now that she was out of shape.

There was a large rock on the beach not too far from the leaders. If she could get to that rock, she could hide behind it and she could hear what they were saying. To get there, though, there was a small stretch of sand where she could be seen if they happened to look her way while she was in view.

Lakali didn't know if she could do this or not. Was she really as brave as she wanted to be? She knew she would be risking her life to get this information. Yet, something inside Lakali told her that her life was in danger anyway. She thought again of the leader coming into her hut and smelling her hair and hearing him say he wanted to take her to his friends. Whatever his purpose was, Lakali knew that wouldn't have been a good thing. Indeed, to protect her future, it seemed like the only possible choice was to risk her life now.

"You can do this," she thought to herself, trying to get the courage she needed to accomplish the task at hand.

Lakali peeked her head out from around the hut. The leaders were all looking out to the ocean. This was her best chance. It was now or never. She held her breath and eased out from behind the hut. She was barefoot, so her feet made little noise as they ran across the sand. When she got to the rock, she collapsed quietly onto the ground, doing all she could to steady her breathing while remaining quiet. She was sure that the leaders would come and find her at any moment. Then, it would be all over for her.

But they didn't come. Every moment that passed, Lakali was amazed to find that she had actually pulled it off.

She had been so fearful and so relieved to be hidden that she hadn't focused on listening. Now, she strained her ears to listen in on their conversation.

Their voices were loud. They weren't concerned about anyone hearing them as this section was now deserted. Even had there been any islanders around, the leaders would have believed that they were under the power of the crystals. They still would have felt free to speak loudly.

Lakali felt brave. Slowly, she moved her head to peek around the side of the rock. She could now see that one of the leaders was holding a large crystal, much larger than the small ones that were placed in the islanders' trinket boxes. It wasn't clear like the other crystals but was a deep purple color. Yet, as it glowed, an array of different colored lights came out from it. Beautiful colors – pink, green, purple, silver, gold. There were so many colors that Lakali couldn't even notice them all. Seeing the crystal, Lakali almost forgot why she was here. Suddenly afraid that this crystal might have even more power over her than her own crystal did, she ducked her head back behind the rock. She didn't know for sure, but she suspected that the crystal the leader was holding was a very powerful and dangerous thing.

She tried to forget about the crystal and instead just listened to what the leaders were saying. She didn't know them by name. In fact, she wouldn't have been able to pick a leader out in a crowd except for the fact that the leaders dressed differently than the islanders. The islanders dressed casual in shorts, halter tops, t-shirts and simple skirts from time to time. Most of the time, the men went without any shirts at all. But the leaders all wore long silver pants and gold slip-over shirts. Their arms and legs were covered. No one ever questioned this. It was just how things were. Everyone assumed the leaders were simply able to handle the warm weather better and didn't mind being covered in so much clothing. The fact that the color and material was so different was assumed to be a way of making the leaders stand out. If someone needed help from someone official, they would want to be able to spot a leader right away.

"How long can you keep that going, Bryayntan?" the first voice asked.

"Long enough, Hakelfard," Bryayntan replied. "You know that I am skilled enough to do this. I can easily keep the crystals activated for a few more hours if needed."

"You're getting good with that thing!" Hakelfard responded.

"Well, I've had centuries to practice!" Bryayntan replied.

"This better work," a third voice said. It

belonged to a leader named Isenviole. "We need more islanders. Their numbers are dropping too rapidly. I am never happy when our supply is under enough to sustain us for at least five years. The young ones aren't populating fast enough to compensate for the losses."

"I am missing our normal session. This had better at least be worth it!" Hakelfard said.

"It will be," Bryayntan replied. "You will be thanking me for this idea come tomorrow when you see our fresh set of islanders, ripe for the taking!"

"Do you think enough time has passed since we last brought in humans?" Isenviole asked. "I remember that day like it was yesterday. When Aarnshire first spotted the ship, it was a glorious day."

"Yes, it was," Aarnshire recalled. "Our numbers were getting much too low. But I do think enough time has passed now. It's the right time to bring more in."

"I'm glad that you agree with me," Bryayntan said. "I like to take care of my friends as much as I like to take care of myself!"

"There are plenty of empty huts now. It is definitely the perfect time to bring more in. Soon, we'll be giving the newcomers new memories," Hakelfard added. "There's no need for them to remember their past lives. They'll believe that they have always lived on this island."

"True," Isenviole replied. "You do think of everything."

"As do we all," Aarnshire replied. "It is a common trait of our species."

"Is the shield to the island down yet?" Hakelfard asked.

"As of five minutes ago," Aarnshire replied. "I spotted a plane heading in from the west. I've already initiated an electrical storm to meet it. They will be looking for a safe place to land."

Lakali was still afraid to look at the leaders for fear of what the crystal might do to her. She didn't see the small crystal in Aarnshire's hand. It was a solid white color and had grey lines woven throughout it. At first glance, it wouldn't seem as powerful as the larger crystal which controlled the clear-thinking sessions. But this crystal held a great power. It could put a shield around the entire island, and it could also interfere with the controls of passing ships and planes.

"Again, you are the one to spot the new islanders for us," Hakelfard replied "You'd better reel them in quickly. They will see that there isn't enough room to land here soon enough."

"I know what I'm doing," Aarnshire said. "Do not worry so!"

High in the sky, the 747 was on its way back to the Mainland from Hawaii, heading back to the state of California. They hadn't been in the air too long and were much closer to the Hawaiian Islands than they were to the mainland, but they had already put substantial distance between themselves and their last location. The pilot advised the passengers to buckle their seatbelts as they were encountering severe turbulence.

The plane wasn't nearly as full as it used to be. The economy had slowed down, and fewer people were going on vacations these days. The pilot wondered how long it would be before the airline cut back on flights once again. He wondered if they would be able to keep him on full-time or if his hours would start to be cut. The plane was only carrying two hundred ten passengers and eight crew members. Suddenly, all thoughts of budget cuts were gone, and the pilot had bigger concerns on his mind.

"What in the world is that?!" the pilot asked, worried.

"I don't like this," the co-pilot said.

But it happened so quickly that there wasn't time to change their course or steer away from it. The electrical storm was all around them, hitting the plane from all directions. It wasn't long before it had taken out two engines.

"Mayday!" the pilot called over the radio.

But to his horror, he discovered that they no longer had any communication systems operable either. The pilot spotted the island, but he couldn't see a safe place to land. He ordered the flight attendants to prepare the passengers for a crash landing. The plane shook and tilted, and none of the controls were working. Suddenly, everything was out of their control. They didn't know that the plane was being controlled from the ground.

On the island, Aarnshire worked with the smaller crystal to bring the plane down. He maneuvered it out of the electrical storm and slowed it down until by the time it approached the island, it was barely moving. He brought the plane down to sit upon the water.

"Quickly!" he commanded the other leaders. "Retrieve the passengers! I can only hold it there so long before it sinks!"

Isenviole and Hakelfard ran to the water. Bryayntan remained focused on his job, using the bigger crystal to keep all of the islanders under the power of their crystals.

Lakali hadn't been able to keep herself from peeking her head out when the excitement began. As she now watched, the leaders were running to the plane. She wasn't sure if she was seeing correctly or not. When they got to the water, it was as if their whole bodies changed, metamorphosing into something else, something fish-like. Once in the water, they made haste and got to the plane in no time.

Lakali and the other islanders had never seen a plane. The electrical storm had blocked her view of seeing it in the sky until it had come along to skim the ocean. She had only seen the last few seconds of it when it was still in the air. She was fascinated and terrified, all at the same time.

When the leaders got to the plane, they signaled Aarnshire to use the crystal to open the emergency exits. Aarnshire did as they instructed. By now, the leaders in the water looked completely human again.

Inside the plane, the passengers were frightened. They were screaming and looking for exits. Inside the plane, it was like its own electrical storm was brewing. Electricity beams shot like lasers over the passengers' heads. The lights in the plane went on and off in rapid succession.

As passengers looked out windows and the emergency exits, no one understood how their plane appeared to be floating on the water. They all expected it to sink and feared that they would drown soon. They looked to the water below. It was surprisingly calm. As the passengers and crew got to the doors, they saw the island and the leaders who were waiting for them in the water. Everything was peaceful outside of the plane. There wasn't a storm cloud in the sky. The only storm was inside the plane! It was spooky, and they all knew something wasn't right. They also knew that they were in trouble.

"Quickly," Isenviole shouted. "Jump! You can swim to shore. My friends and I will help you!"

The passengers were frightened, but they

knew they didn't have any choice. They couldn't stay in this deathtrap. They jumped into the water, many carrying their flotation devices. Slowly but surely, they all got off the plane and found their way to shore.

Lakali was breathing hard by now. She hurried and ran back to hide behind a hut. The beach was filling up too fast. She would be easy to spot by the leaders as most of the passengers were dressed differently. Some wore long jackets and pants. Even the ones wearing shorts and simple tops still looked to be dressed differently than her. Their brightly-colored fabrics and patterns contrasted with the plain clothing that the islanders wore.

Who were all these people anyway? Where had they come from? Sure, Lakali had seen the plane, but she didn't know what it was or how it had even gotten there. She could feel her heart racing.

Even from the distance where she stood, Lakali could see some of what was happening on shore. Isenviole and Hakelfard had come onto the beach now. They were handing out trinket boxes. Each person who got a box opened it, as instructed by the leaders. Once the boxes were open, even from here, Lakali could see that they contained crystals. She was careful not to look directly at them. Once the people looked upon the crystals, Lakali could see the familiar dazed looks.

There were a few children also. The children looked frightened, but they were ushered to an empty hut. Isenviole locked the door behind them. Apparently, they wouldn't be going to the playground today.

Lakali carefully followed some of the people who were being led by Hakelfard, being careful to stay hidden and remain at a distance. She watched as they were escorted to their huts.

At one point, Lakali barely got behind a hut in time before being spotted. She listened as Hakelfard instructed the young man who had just been led to his new home.

"Here is where you will live," Hakelfard said. "You will keep this trinket box in your hut at all times, and you will guard it with your life. You must never, ever let anything happen to it. Do you understand?"

Lakali couldn't hear any response, but she assumed that he must have nodded when she heard Hakelfard respond with, "Very well. Welcome to our island. I am sure you will be very happy here. We will get you more appropriate clothing by morning."

Lakali stayed where she was, too afraid to move or do anything. When she felt it was safe, she poked her head around the hut. It finally looked like all of the people had been placed in huts. The leaders were the only ones remaining. Quietly, she slipped out from behind the hut and ran to one that was closer to where the leaders were standing. It was too dangerous to risk going back to the rock where she first hid, but the leaders were closer to her now and she was convinced that their loud voices would carry to the hut she was hiding behind.

"How much longer, Bryayntan?" Hakelfard asked.

"Just a few more minutes until their previous memories are erased," Bryayntan replied. "It takes a few minutes seeing how I have to keep the clear-thinking session going also."

A few more minutes passed.

"There!" Aarnshire said. "Now, all that anyone will see as they pass our island will be intense storm clouds and lightning, enough so that no one will want to come anywhere near us."

He had been working on putting the island's shield back up.

"Of course, if they were to be so stupid, their planes and ships would hit our force field. Then, they would crash and sink," he added. "None of our concern anyway!"

"It would seem like a waste, though," Isenviole replied. "Don't you think so, Bryayntan?"

"Don't disturb him," Aarnshire scolded. "Not until their memories are erased!

"It's okay," Bryayntan replied. "The crystals have been working long enough. The newcomers' memories are gone by now, for sure. And yes, I suppose it would be a waste if any planes crashed. But like Aarnshire said, it's not our concern anyway."

"Let's just finish up here," Hakelfard responded. "I'm feeling rather exhausted."

"I agree. We must get this done as quickly as possible," Aarnshire said. "We must seal all their doors until we can go in and speak to each person. We will plant new memories, and then they can come out. It's going to be a busy afternoon. As soon as their doors are sealed, Bryayntan can end the clear-thinking session. Then, we'll take turns standing guard to make sure no one else comes near here. It shouldn't be an issue. No work duty has been assigned in this section today."

Bryayntan still held the large crystal. All of the leaders had a lot of practice with it. They took turns controlling the clear-thinking sessions. They were so skilled at it that they could easily converse while keeping the sessions going. A job like today that also required the erasing of many memories was more complex. But now that that part was done, the rest would be easy.

"Isenviole and Hakelfard, help me secure the huts," Aarnshire instructed.

"Let's get to it!" Hakelfard responded.

Lakali watched as they headed to a hut in a direction opposite of where she was hiding. She knew she had to get out of there, and this was her chance. They would be coming back to seal the huts she was near soon. She darted from hut to hut, making sure she had cover until she knew she was out of sight. Then, she ran for all she worth back to Section Five.

Chapter 11

Lakali was breathless by the time she reached her section. She stopped and put her hands on her knees as she knelt slightly, trying to catch her breath. She knew she couldn't stay in that position for long, though, as she saw the islanders start to emerge from their huts. She knew that she must hurry.

It was only a few more minutes until she approached her hut. She saw Akoni with his hand on the knob, poised to open the door.

"No!" she thought to herself, knowing that she had left the trinket box open. No islander was ever to leave the box open except for during the clear-thinking sessions.

"Akoni!" Lakali shouted and drew his attention away from the door. "I'm over here!"

She was only a couple of huts away from him. She walked quickly to close the distance between herself and Akoni.

"What are you doing out here?" Akoni asked, confused.

"I came out before you did," Lakali answered, not telling him *how* long she had been out of her hut.

"I thought I came out as soon as the session was over," Akoni questioned.

"I guess you're slower than you thought you were," Lakali stated.

By now, she had reached Akoni. She put her arms around his waist and drew him to her. She gave him a long kiss. There was one way to distract Akoni from his thoughts, and Lakali was very good at providing distractions.

"Want to go for a swim?" Lakali asked.

"With you?" Akoni asked. "Anytime!"

"Go and wait for me in the water," Lakali said. "I'll put my swimwear on."

"Don't be long," Akoni whispered as he reached down to kiss Lakali on the neck. "I get restless when I'm away from you for too long."

"I'll be quick. I promise," Lakali replied.

They withdrew their hold on each other, and Lakali watched as Akoni walked away. He was shirtless and was wearing shorts that could easily double as swimwear. He headed straight for the water.

When she was sure no one was looking, Lakali quickly opened the door of her hut and darted in, half-expecting to see the glow of the crystal. But now that the clear-thinking session had ended, there was no need to worry. The crystal sat in the box, looking completely harmless. She quickly rushed to the box and closed the lid, returning it to its place on the shelf.

She took time to take a deep breath and let it out. That had been a close call. Plus, she was still shaken up by what she had seen. She thought of the images she had seen – the strange metallic object floating on the water, all of the people who came from its belly, the leaders who had gone into the water and changed forms before her very eyes. Lakali began to question if she had really seen the things she had seen. It was crazy to think it had been real, but she was not one to give way to hallucinations. She knew that she had seen and heard everything correctly, but she couldn't make any sense of it. Were their leaders some sort of monsters? It seemed so ludicrous to even think such a thing. And yet, what else could she think?

The strange comments made by the leaders upset her also. They spoke of a five-year supply. What did that mean? Lakali had some ideas, but she refused to let her mind think such frightening thoughts.

At the very least, she now knew for sure that their leaders couldn't be trusted. She had heard with her very own ears as they spoke of planting false memories in the new islanders' heads. Those people who had come to the island would soon not even know who they were.

Lakali had a thought so disturbing, she had to try to push it out of her mind. What if her memories were false? What if she was remembering things that weren't real? What if she, too, had not always lived on the island?

How could the leaders so heartlessly erase people's memories?

Amzi! No wonder Caristiona and Akoni couldn't remember him! Their memories had been erased by their leaders. She was the only one who could remember Amzi, and it was all because of the crystals. Once she became strong enough to not succumb to her crystal's power, it was no longer able to alter her memories. But the other islanders weren't so fortunate. Lakali wondered if anyone else was strong enough to resist the power of the crystals. Could anyone else remember Amzi?

Somehow, Lakali didn't think so, but she would test her theory later and throw his name around to the people in her section. She wouldn't indicate it was anyone who they *should* know, but rather just throw his name out there and see what their reactions were. If there was even a small chance that someone else was awake and not under the power of the crystals, she had to know!

Lakali thought again about her crystal. Most

likely, she was the only islander who had stopped looking at it during the clear-thinking sessions. Whatever power it held over the islanders, Lakali knew it was because of their leaders. She also believed that it must be connected in some way to the other larger crystal she had seen. That must be how memories were planted and erased. She knew now more than ever that she must never allow her eyes to rest upon the crystal once the clear-thinking sessions began. It was imperative that she stay awake and alert. She could feel something bad was coming. The only way to fight it would be if she could stay awake.

She thought again about the leader who had come into her hut and had lifted her hair to smell it. What had he wanted with her? He had mentioned he wanted to take her to his friends, but why? Surely, by now, if they knew she was no longer under the power of the crystal, they would have dealt with her. No, it was something else they wanted, and she suspected it had something to do with that five-year supply the leaders were talking about.

She shuddered. It was hard to not physically shake. She knew she had to come up with a plan. If she just sat around and did nothing, she had a sinking feeling that she would soon be the one to go missing. Only no one would miss her. Any memory of her would be erased from the other islanders' thoughts. Even her devoted Akoni who had said that someday he would marry her would no longer remember her.

Lakali was surprised to feel a tear slipping down her cheek. Somehow, the thought of Akoni forgetting her upset her even worse than the thought of dying. She couldn't let any of this happen. If the crystals held power over the islanders, then she had to do something to keep the others from looking at their crystals. But what?

Time was slipping away. Soon, Akoni would come looking for her. She quickly got dressed and headed for the beach. All the while, her mind was racing, thinking of what she could do to break the power that the crystals held over the islanders.

As Lakali walked to the beach, she began to devise a plan. She must get into Akoni's hut when he went to work the next day. She would open his box and steal the crystal. She would only tell him when he returned that he mustn't look inside his trinket box and that he mustn't let anyone else know that he was aware of anything going on around him once the clear-thinking session began. She didn't want him to see that his crystal was missing, but she also didn't want him walking around looking awake. She would instruct him to go into his hut when he saw the other islanders heading to their clear-thinking sessions.

Of course, Akoni would probably threaten to go to the leaders and ask them to help Lakali. He would tell Lakali that she was talking crazy, but she would beg him to give her just one afternoon. If he still felt the same way the next day, she would turn herself in. He would feel so sorry for her as she cried that she could convince him. At least, that was what she hoped would happen.

Akoni saw Lakali coming into the water. She looked lovely in her two-piece swimwear. He smiled and made a kissing sound at her.

"You sure know how to keep a guy waiting, don't you?" he called to her.

She went to him, and they embraced each other. The water came up to their waists. Akoni pulled Lakali close and leaned down to kiss her. They stayed that way for a long time, holding each other and kissing. Lakali tried to focus on Akoni and returned his kisses, but her mind was reeling. She wondered if she could pull off her plan the next day.

Akoni could sense that he didn't have Lakali's full attention. There was something bothering his girlfriend, but he knew she wouldn't tell him. He thought of going to the leaders to ask for help, but he knew that would only upset her more. He would have to keep an eye on her. He pushed those thoughts out of his head and drew her closer, trying to focus only on the softness of her lips and her body next to his.

Lakali mentioned none of her concerns to Akoni for the rest of the evening. He could tell there was something she wasn't telling him, but he didn't press her for information. The next morning, he went off on a hunting expedition. His group was looking for native birds the leaders had named Starfeathers. They were known to be an island delicacy. They were beautiful birds. The sunlight shone off of their feathers, thus giving them their name. However, the birds were hard to get and rarely did a hunting expedition come home with any of the favored food. Other less-tasty birds were in more abundance. Most likely, that was what they would be bringing back today.

Lakali had a shift working with the laundry and was at the stream scrubbing clothes. She was happy to see that Bakita had also been assigned to do the laundry with her.

"So, how is Hachuo?" Lakali asked. "As demanding as ever?"

Bakita laughed.

"Oh, he just likes to give me a hard time, to get me going. It makes for a fun argument, you know?" Bakita replied. "I just give it right back to him!"

"Of that, I'm sure," Lakali said.

"Speaking of impossible men, what about Akoni?" Bakita asked. "Has he even mentioned putting a ring on your finger yet?"

"As a matter of fact..." Lakali answered.

"What?!" Bakita exclaimed. "Why on earth didn't you say something?"

"We haven't seen each other for a while, remember?" Lakali replied. "Besides, it's not official yet. He just said that he does plan to marry me."

"Harrumph!" Bakita scoffed. "Those are just words that are meant to string a pretty girl along. You tell him that it's time to get serious. You are a woman now. It's time for you to settle down and make little Lakalis and Akonis."

Lakali blushed.

"I could never be so demanding of him," she said. "But if I were, I am sure he would agree to marry me at once."

"Then, you must become demanding!" Bakita replied. "It's the only way!"

"I'll think on it," Lakali said.

"Don't think. Do!" Bakita insisted.

"Okay, I promise to try," Lakali answered.

They sat in silence for a few moments as they scrubbed the shirts in their buckets. Finally, Lakali got up the nerve to ask the question for which she so desperately needed an answer.

"By the way," Lakali began. "Have you ever heard of a boy named Amzi?"

Bakita stopped scrubbing and looked at Lakali. She appeared to be a bit confused.

"Amzi?" she asked, and Lakali could see that Bakita was trying to search her memories.

"Hmmm," Bakita finally answered. "I don't think I know any Amzi, although I have to admit that the name has a certain familiarity to it. Who is he? Is he someone of importance?"

"No, I don't think so," Lakali replied. "He's just a boy I heard about who lives over in Section Three. I was told that he looked like a younger version of Hachuo, and I thought you might find that amusing. I figured if you knew him, you could tell me if it was true and if he really does look like your husband, only younger."

Bakita laughed.

"I barely remember what Hachuo looked like twenty years ago when we first met. I don't know if I would even recognize the similarities. I've gotten quite used to his grey hairs and wrinkles," she said. "Still, it would be interesting to meet this Amzi and see if I could spot any resemblances."

"Yes, it would," Lakali agreed.

Lakali knew that Bakita had known of Amzi. She was also good friends with Caristiona. There were many nights they had all spent having dinner together, six of them in all as Hachuo, Amzi, and Akoni had joined them.

What had she been thinking? No one remembered Amzi except for Lakali. This reinforced her theory that it was because she was the only one who was no longer looking at her crystal during their clear-thinking sessions.

She did find it interesting that the name sounded familiar to Bakita. Surely, there was some part of her mind that retained the memory of Amzi. It was just too weak to pull the memory out. Lakali wondered if there could be a way to bring the memory back. If Bakita didn't have her crystal, would the memories come back, or were they hidden in the recesses of her mind forever?

When their work was done, the ladies bid each other farewell and Lakali hurried back to her hut. She was worried that the laundry had taken too long and that Akoni might have gotten home before her. She was very relieved when she got back to her hut and didn't see Akoni anywhere. She returned the laundry to the wash hut. That was where people left their clothing and came to retrieve it when it was done. Then, she hurried back to Akoni's hut. She looked around. Everyone seemed busy and occupied. She should be able to sneak into Akoni's hut if she hurried.

Much to Lakali's relief, there was no sign of Akoni. He hadn't returned from work yet. Lakali took a deep breath and held it as she opened the door and rushed inside. She quickly went to his trinket box and opened the lid. She looked at the crystal inside and wondered how something that could become so beautiful could also be so evil.

Pushing those thoughts from her mind, she grabbed the crystal and placed it in the pocket of her shorts. She would keep her hand in the pocket, hoping that no one would notice the small bulge that the crystal made.

Lakali closed the box and returned it to its spot. Just having the crystal on her made Lakali feel weird. It was like the crystal knew it was being moved and didn't want to leave its spot. She began to feel dizzy. For a moment, she thought she might black out. She took a few deep breaths, exhaling slowly and then pulled herself together.

She exited the hut and walked quickly toward the ocean. She wanted to run, but her body wouldn't cooperate. There was definitely something happening with the crystal. It was as if it had some sort of connection to the box and was trying to stop her from going any further. It took all the physical strength she could muster to keep moving forward, one step at a time.

"Lakali!" she heard Akoni calling her, but Lakali couldn't turn around now. She couldn't be distracted.

The weight of the crystal in her pocket was too much, and she felt like collapsing on the sand. She knew she had to finish the job and get rid of the crystal as quickly as possible. She ignored Akoni and continued walking to the beach. She could still hear Akoni calling her, and his voice was getting closer.

Lakali plunged ahead until she was in the water. She looked down at her pocket where the crystal was, almost expecting it to be glowing. But there was no sign of it, and no one seemed to be paying any attention to what she was doing except for Akoni.

Lakali continued into the water. She had to be far enough out for her pocket to be hidden. The further out, the better. Lakali almost wondered if the crystal would have the power to return itself to Akoni's box.

"Lakali!"

Akoni was getting much too close. Lakali wanted to look back, but she knew she didn't dare. She had to get rid of the crystal before Akoni got to her. She was now waist-high in the water. A few more steps should do it. When the water was up to her chest, Lakali reached into her pocket and pulled out the crystal, grasping it tightly and then letting it slip into the water. Almost afraid the crystal would float, she turned to head back to shore. Only as she turned, Akoni was right there.

"What are you doing?" Akoni asked. "Didn't you hear me call?"

"No," Lakali lied.

"But I was right behind you!" Akoni insisted. "Surely, you heard me!"

Lakali knew she needed to get out of the ocean. Not knowing if the crystal would float or sink, she couldn't risk Akoni seeing it.

"Let's go back to shore," she said, and Lakali turned Akoni to face the huts.

The crystal was weighted down by its foreign elements inside. Even though she wasn't able to witness it for herself, it sank slowly to the sand below, emitting a very faint green glow as it went down to find its resting place.

As they walked toward the shore, Akoni moved slowly.

"You're not making any sense," he said. "I saw you walking with such urgency and completely ignoring me. You didn't even take time to put on your swimwear. You're wearing your everyday clothes. You never go swimming without your swimwear. And now, you suddenly want to turn and go back to shore? None of this makes sense, Lakali. Speak to me!"

"I will," Lakali said. "I promise. But we need privacy."

"There's no one within hearing range," Akoni replied, looking around and seeing no one near them. "We can speak here."

"I'd be much more comfortable in my hut," Lakali insisted.

"I don't understand you sometimes," Akoni said. "I hope you will offer me a full explanation when we get to your hut."

"I promise," Lakali said. "I will tell you everything."

They walked toward Lakali's hut. All the while, Lakali tugged on Akoni, trying to get him away from the beach as quickly as possible. When they got to her hut, they went inside and sat on the cot.

"I need you to be open-minded," Lakali said. "What I'm about to tell you will sound too fabulous to believe, but it's all true."

"Go on," Akoni said.

Lakali took a deep breath and then began telling Akoni her crazy story. She told him about how she had learned to not look at the crystal during the clear-thinking sessions and about following the leader to Section Six. She also told him about watching as the humans came in a great metallic object that floated upon the water but looked like no ship she had ever seen. She repeated the conversations she had heard about the leaders erasing the newcomers' memories and implanting false ones. Finally, she told him about the vague comment about a "five-year supply."

All the while Lakali was talking, Akoni sat speechless with his mouth open. Was Lakali crazy? It was true what she had said. Indeed, this story *was* too fabulous to believe.

"Lakali, have you not been feeling well?" Akoni asked. "Are you not sleeping well at night?"

"I knew you wouldn't believe me," Lakali said, feeling completely alone.

"It's not that I don't want to believe you," Akoni said, seeing how upset she was. "But you have to admit, this story sounds crazy!"

"I know it does," Lakali replied. "But why would I make up something like that?"

"I didn't say you were making it up," Akoni answered. "I think you do believe it. But Lakali, none of that can be true. Our leaders have always taken care of us. They help us with anything we need. Surely, if we were to go to them together, they could figure out why you are having these false memories!"

"No!" Lakali said. "Unless you want to be responsible for my death, you must not talk to them about me. They'll kill me, Akoni!"

"That's ridiculous, Lakali," Akoni insisted. "They'll want to help."

"You mustn't!" Lakali began to cry.

Akoni felt bad for her. He hated to see her cry. He drew her into his arms to comfort her.

"It's okay," he said. "I won't say anything. I promise."

Lakali sat up and wiped her eyes, but she continued to sniffle.

"You're the only person I truly have," Lakali said. "Caristiona thinks I'm crazy. I can't lose you!"

"You're not going to lose me," Akoni replied.

"But you'll forget me, just like Caristiona forgot Amzi," she insisted.

"I could never forget you, Lakali," Akoni said sincerely. "I'm in love with you."

"But you will," Lakali replied. "When I go missing, you'll forget all about me. I'm telling you that our leaders are making us forget people!"

She realized that she was practically shouting. She made a point to lower her voice.

"We can't trust them, Akoni," Lakali started to cry. "And what about your parents? Don't you want to remember them?"

"Lakali, you know that my mom died in childbirth," Akoni said. "My father was so heartbroken that he drowned himself in the ocean."

"How do you know that's true?" Lakali asked. "It wasn't like you would be able to remember on your own. He killed himself before you were old enough to remember him."

"It's what I was always told," Akoni answered.

"And by who?" Lakali asked.

"Lakali, this is crazy," Akoni said. "Our leaders aren't erasing our memories!"

"Then, what about my parents?" Lakali asked. "How convenient it is that neither of us remember our own families!"

"I never knew your parents, but you heard the stories," Akoni replied. "They were on the fishing boat and had a terrible accident. The leaders told you that the trauma was too much for you and it made you forget them. It happens sometimes. Eventually, maybe you'll remember them. But that doesn't mean that the leaders had anything to do with their deaths."

"You promised me you would be open-minded," Lakali reminded him.

"Yes, but you are speaking crazy," Akoni said. "You need to take a nap. You'll think more clearly after you get some rest. By the way, you never explained to me why you were rushing to the water today while you were still fully-clothed. What was all that about anyway? Why were you ignoring me?"

Lakali took a deep breath and let it out slowly. She knew that Akoni wouldn't like what she was about to tell him, and she needed his cooperation. She was afraid he would never agree, and she didn't know if she could keep him from going to talk to the leaders about her.

"What?" Akoni asked. "What is it?"

"You have to hear me out," Lakali said. "You have to promise you won't just get mad at me, but that we will discuss this."

"Lakali!" Akoni said, now getting annoyed. "Just tell me, what was that all about?"

"I had to take care of something. I had to leave it in the ocean," Lakali replied.

"Just *what* did you leave in the ocean?" Akoni asked, now suspicious and more worried than ever.

Lakali hesitated and sucked in some air to get her courage before answering.

"Your crystal," Lakali finally answered.

"What?!" Akoni shouted angrily. "What were

you thinking?!"

"Akoni, it has you under its power," she replied. "I had to do something to wake you up!"

"We are to guard those crystals with our lives!" Akoni said. "What am I going to do? How am I ever going to explain this to the leaders?"

"They don't have to know," Lakali answered.

"Well, if the story you told me is true, apparently they come around and check," Akoni answered.

"You can block your door," Lakali said. "They'll get frustrated and move on, but they won't think you blocked it purposely. They don't have any reason to suspect you."

"And the next day?" Akoni asked. "I block it then, too? Won't they become suspicious then?"

"Oh, Akoni, I didn't think of that!" Lakali began to sob.

"Why would you do this?!" Akoni shouted angrily.

"I was worried about you," Lakali cried. "I was just trying to help. I didn't think it all through clearly enough. I just needed for you to wake up!"

"Maybe if you hadn't been keeping yourself from your clear-thinking sessions, none of this would have happened!" Akoni snapped. "This is all crazy. I have to go get the crystal!"

"Akoni, please! Whatever you do, don't look at it!" Lakali begged as Akoni went rushing to the ocean, looking for the approximate spot where Lakali had gone.

As he swam out into the ocean, Akoni gauged when he was at about the same depth where he had caught up with Lakali. He held his breath and ducked down into the water, trying to see and search the ocean floor. After about fifteen minutes, he was almost ready to give up. He would have to go to the leaders and tell them that Lakali was sick. Surely, they wouldn't be angry when they saw that she was mentally ill. They would know how to help her. He dreaded what he had to do, but he couldn't be without his crystal. He had to trust his leaders. He went down for one more search, and that was when he saw a faint green glow coming from the ocean floor about twenty feet in front of him.

Akoni swam quickly. When he came to the crystal, he scooped it up. He held it tightly and felt relieved. He brought his head above water, his hand latched onto the crystal as he made his way to shore. He could feel the weight of the crystal in his hand. It was slowing him down. But he noticed that the closer he got to his hut, the lighter the crystal became.

Lakali was watching him from her doorway. He could see that she was crying, but he ignored her as he went into his hut and replaced the crystal in his trinket box.

He had barely begun to replace it and close the lid to the trinket box when he began to feel an urge to sit down and look upon the crystal. His mind wasn't as strong as Lakali's. He didn't know if he could resist, but he kept saying the words over and over in his head, somehow having to prove to himself beyond a shadow of a doubt that his girlfriend was indeed crazy.

"Don't look at the crystal! Don't look at the crystal!" he said silently to himself.

If he could do this and not look at the crystal this one time, then he could tell Lakali he had tried and she would surely see that she was wrong.

Akoni felt as if his head was about to explode. The pressure was building up. It was so intense that it was almost too much for him to handle. Again, Akoni wondered if he was strong enough to pull this off. It would be so easy to just look. What had Lakali said? That's right. She had said that she looked just above the rim of the box.

"Focus! Focus! You can do this!" Akoni thought to himself.

He was about to give up and look at the crystal when he heard the knob on his door turn. From the corner of his eye, he could see the leader look in just like Lakali told him would happen. The leader saw the glow from the crystal and saw Akoni staring without expression into the box. At least, that was what it appeared like to him. He had no idea that Akoni was awake and that he was watching him from the corner of his eye.

Akoni became nervous and moved just slightly. The leader had been about to leave, but now he stopped. He had to make sure that Akoni was truly under the power of the crystal. He remained in the doorway and stared at Akoni. Sitting on the floor, Akoni became more frightened. He could feel how closely he was being observed. He toyed with the idea of talking to the leader and telling him about Lakali and asking him to help her, but he felt too uneasy. He didn't know if the leader could be trusted or not. This was all so crazy. Now, Lakali was filling his mind with crazy thoughts also! He was about to give up and confess that he was awake when the leader turned and left the hut, convinced that Akoni was in a trance like all of the other islanders.

When the leader left, Akoni released his breath, not even having realized he had been holding it. He knew when the clear-thinking session ended because the crystal stopped glowing. He rushed to Lakali's hut to see if she was alright. When he entered, she threw her arms around him and hugged him tight.

"Oh, Akoni, I was so worried!" she said. "I didn't know what you were going to do!"

"It's okay. I'm alright," Akoni said. "Nothing bad happened."

"I wish you would have believed me," Lakali cried. "I needed you to see for yourself that I was telling the truth."

"I was awake," Akoni replied. "I did as you told me. I didn't look at the crystal. I was awake the whole time."

Lakali looked up at Akoni.

"Oh, Akoni!" she said. "You trusted me. Now, you know that I'm telling the truth!"

"I don't know anything," Akoni replied. "All I saw was the leader coming in just like you said he would. He stayed there for a few minutes to make sure I wasn't awake. It doesn't mean anything."

"Of course it does," Lakali said. "Why are they so concerned to make sure none of us are awake?"

"It's because they want us to think clearly," Akoni answered.

"When the leader was in your doorway, how did you feel?" Lakali asked.

"Scared," Akoni replied. "But that was surely because of all the crazy things you told me. I really had no reason to fear him."

"Sometimes, you have to listen to your heart," Lakali said. "What is your heart telling you? Before you answer, take a moment to really listen to it."

Akoni went to the cot and sat down. After a couple of minutes, he spoke.

"I don't know," he said. "I just don't know."

"Talk to me," Lakali urged.

"Well, I don't want to believe any of this," Akoni said. "It's all too frightening."

"But?" Lakali asked.

"I don't know," Akoni answered. "There was

something about the way he was watching me. It kind of made my skin crawl."

"See?!" Lakali replied. "I told you!"

"I'm not sure I see anything yet," Akoni said.

"You have to try," Lakali insisted. "Until you are sure of how you feel, you must promise me you will continue to not look at the crystal during the clear-thinking sessions."

"I don't know," Akoni replied.

"Please, Akoni!" Lakali begged. "We've come too far to give up now. You did it today. You can continue to do it. We'll get to the bottom of whatever is happening. I promise!"

Akoni looked at Lakali. Now, he didn't know what to believe. One thing was for sure. Lakali truly believed the story she was telling him. Could it be true? Could she have seen all the crazy things she claimed to have seen?

"I'll try," Akoni promised, resolving himself to stay awake again tomorrow.

Chapter 12

When they both got back from work the next day, Lakali kept reminding Akoni to be strong and to stay awake. She knew the crystal would pull at him, urging him to look upon it and put him under its power. Akoni promised he would try to not look at it. He kept repeating the words to himself.

"Don't look at the crystal! Don't look at the crystal!"

He thought he must be crazy. He had even agreed to wait until their huts had been cleared and to go with Lakali to spy on their leaders. He had wanted to see for himself what they were up to, if anything. He was already kicking himself for agreeing. He couldn't really believe the things Lakali had told him. He was amazed at what he could let that girl talk him into doing.

Akoni's heart was racing as he heard the door to his hut open once the clear-thinking session had begun. He told himself to keep a straight face and to not let the leader see that he was awake. He was looking just over the rim of the box as he had done yesterday. Again, the crystal pulled at him, urging him to look at it. Again, his head felt like it could explode.

When the door opened, to Akoni's horror, the leader entered the hut. He came and stood behind Akoni, then circling him as if checking him closely.

"I've got one," Hakelfard shouted loudly.

Akoni started to tremble. He didn't know what was happening, but he knew that he was in trouble. Hakelfard reached down and grabbed Akoni, the box and crystal falling away from him as he did so. Hakelfard knew that Akoni was now awake. The humans always woke up when they were selected. Akoni tried to resist, but Hakelfard was so strong, way stronger than any person Akoni had ever encountered. Hakelfard yanked him toward the door.

"What are you doing?" Akoni asked in a frightened voice. "Where are you taking me?"

"You'll find out soon enough!" Hakelfard said and laughed.

"Stop! No!" Akoni shouted as he was dragged outside.

Awake in her hut, Lakali heard the commotion. She could hear Akoni screaming and shouting and telling someone to stop. She started to get up to see what was happening, but she heard her door start to open. She quickly put herself back into position and stared intently in front of her, just over the rim of the box. It was the same leader who had come into her hut the other day, Isenviole. He came in and again stood behind Lakali. Once again, he pulled up her hair to sniff it. Lakali focused on steadying her breathing and remained stoic, not allowing Isenviole to see that she was awake. All the while, she could hear Akoni screaming.

"It's too bad my friend has already selected someone else," Isenviole said. "I was looking forward to bringing you to them today. Tomorrow, you will be mine."

He turned and left, hurrying out of the hut. When he was gone, Lakali started gasping for breath. She felt like she was going to hyperventilate, but there was no time for her to waste. She rushed from her place on the mat and opened the door much too quickly, not even caring if she was risking being spotted. Fortunately, Isenviole had already cleared much space between them. He was following along behind Akoni and Hakelfard. Lakali could see Akoni being dragged against his will up the shoreline. She rushed from her hut and followed as quickly as she could. She had barely gotten to the edge of her section when she saw that the other two leaders were there also. They greeted Hakelfard, as he dragged Akoni closer to them.

"It looks like you brought us a tasty one today!" Aarnshire said. "There's enough meat on him to feed us good."

Aarnshire licked his lips and could almost taste the flesh of the human in his mouth as he spoke the words. Akoni was terrified. So, this was their plan. He was to be a meal.

"Are you crazy?!" he shouted. "Let me go! The others will be missing me! You can't just kill me like this!"

"No one will miss you," Aarnshire assured him. "As we speak, your memory is being erased from their minds."

Lakali was now close enough to hear them. She was hiding behind a shack that held wood for their bonfires. Isenviole began to sense that he was being watched. He looked Lakali's way. She ducked her head out of view just in time.

"What is it?" Hakelfard asked.

"Nothing," Isenviole said after a few seconds. "It must have just been the wind playing tricks on me."

"You did check that all of the islanders were asleep?" Aarnshire inquired.

"Of course," Isenviole replied. "I saw no signs of trouble."

"Good, very good," Aarnshire responded. "I'm quite hungry! Let's get this over with."

Akoni was still trying to resist, but he couldn't stop the leaders as three of them dragged him toward the ocean. Lakali peeked out from the shack and could see that Bryayntan was still on the sand, holding the purple crystal.

"Hurry!" he called after his friends. "And don't forget to save some meat for me! I have handled the crystal for three days in a row now. Tomorrow, I get to feed first!"

"No problem," Aarnshire called back.

When they got to the water, the three leaders suddenly metamorphosed into something unhuman. Their bodies became fish-like and covered in scales. Their heads resembled a great puffer fish, and their giant eyes glowed green in the daylight. Their arms and legs became as reptile legs. Akoni screamed in horror.

Lakali knew she had to do something. She looked into the shack and selected a large piece of firewood. Without giving any regard to her own safety, she ran from her hiding place and rushed at Bryayntan who was sitting on the sand. He turned to face her just in time to see the large stick come down and hit him on the top of his head.

When Lakali attacked him, the leader looked completely human, but as the blow struck down upon him, his body changed into the strange fish and reptile-like creature that his friends had also just changed into. As he did so, his eyes glowed green. Giant fin-like skin expanded outward on the sides of his face, and he made a loud hissing sound. He dropped the purple crystal and let out a horrified shrill scream. The scream was so loud that it was almost deafening, and it was Lakali's instinct to cover her ears. But she couldn't be distracted. She knew she must kill him quickly.

The three leaders had just gotten Akoni underwater when they heard the call of distress. Knowing that something was seriously wrong with their friend, they immediately released Akoni and put their heads above water. Upon seeing their friend on the ground, they rushed from the ocean and headed to help him, returning to human form as their reptilian feet hit the sand. Lakali was still standing over the leader, striking him again and again. She stopped to see the other leaders rushing toward her. Panicking, she dropped the stick and ran toward the tree line to get away.

By now, Bryayntan had fallen over backwards and was lying on the ground, his vision getting blurry.

Akoni could see what was happening. He knew that Lakali was in trouble. He wanted to rush to her, but he knew he was outnumbered. If he ran toward the shore, he would be killed. He swam eastward, away from the leaders and in the same general direction that he could see Lakali running. When he had cleared enough space between himself and the leaders, he made a beeline for the shore. He ran as fast as he could, continuing eastward for a short time until he finally headed for the trees to where he had seen Lakali retreat.

The leaders were distracted, trying to take care of their friend. But it became evident soon enough that he was dying and was beyond their help.

Lakali had been running close to the edge of the trees. To her relief, she saw that Akoni was running for safety. She glanced behind and saw that the leaders were giving up on saving their friend. They would surely come after her and Akoni now. She ran to greet Akoni as he reached the trees. Taking no time to talk, they made eye contact and continued running through the trees, trying to put as much distance between themselves and their leaders as possible.

The leaders watched as Akoni entered the trees. They caught a glimpse of Lakali meeting him. Furious, they gave one last look to Bryayntan and saw the light purple blood leaking from his head. Aarnshire went to pick up the crystal and held it over his dying friend. Bryayntan's body began to tremble and suddenly went into wild convulsions. After a few moments, his head began to shrivel up and his body fell into a thousand or more pieces that all started to sink into the sand below him.

"Aarnshire, can you control the islanders and still use the crystal against our enemies?" Isenviole asked.

"I'll do my best," Aarnshire replied.

"But the islanders will be awake," Hakelfard said. "When Bryayntan lost the crystal, that surely released them from their trances."

"I'll do another clear-thinking session," Aarnshire replied. "The islanders won't even realize that they had two sessions today. We do not need anyone else awake while we deal with these two!"

Lakali and Akoni looked back to shore and saw Aarnshire holding the crystal. Oh, if only they had been able to confiscate that! Lakali wanted to kick herself. How had she been so stupid? She had been focusing on killing the leader when her priority should have been on that crystal!

There were now three leaders left. Aarnshire was busy handling the crystal. Isenviole and Hakelfard were trying to decide what to do.

"Maybe we can still catch them," Isenviole suggested.

"Perhaps, but we must be fast," Hakelfard replied.

Without another word, Hakelfard and Isenviole took off running, pursuing Lakali and Akoni.

"Run for all you're worth," Akoni shouted.

There was no need to tell Lakali that!

Lakali and Akoni ran faster than they ever had in their lives as they darted between trees, changing direction from time to time to throw their pursuers off and confuse them. The two leaders chased after them, but Akoni and Lakali had gotten too much of a head start. There were too many trees, and the leaders didn't know which way the couple had gone.

They were angry, but they gave up. They hurried back toward Aarnshire, yelling to him when they had cleared clear the tree line.

"Do it! Now!" Hakelfard shouted.

"Waste no time! They're getting away!" Isenviole added.

As soon as the two leaders were safely out of the trees, Aarnshire saw his chance. He was the most talented of all the leaders when it came to handling the crystal. If any of them could pull this off, it was him. Still concentrating on keeping the islanders under a trance, he willed the crystal to take down the trees and expose Lakali and Akoni.

As they ran, Lakali and Akoni heard a great roar behind them and looked back to see trees crashing down behind them. As the trees collapsed, it was like a domino effect, with the trees coming toward them, getting closer and closer.

At the last minute, they looked to their left and spotted a small cave hidden behind the thickest part of the tree line. They ran to it and darted in just in time before the trees came crashing down around them. It was a very small cave. The entrance was barely visible before the trees collapsed. Now, it would be next to impossible for anyone to see it or its occupants with all of the fallen trees around them.

For a moment, Lakali and Akoni panicked. Perhaps they were trapped in the cave with no way out. But as they looked closer, there appeared to be a very small opening, just big enough for them to crawl out when the time was right. For now, they satisfied themselves with being hidden and held each other tightly as they tried to take small, quiet breaths. If they could just stay hidden long enough, they could escape to safety once their leaders gave up on finding them.

After a couple of minutes, the noise died down. No more trees were falling. The leaders had given up on exposing the two of them so easily. They couldn't take out every tree on the island. Any more, and it would become suspicious. As it was, they would have to plant memories into the islanders' minds of a terrible storm that came through and destroyed so many trees. Aarnshire went to work planting the memories while the other two leaders paced back and forth, not knowing what to do.

"How is it that the girl was awake anyway?" Hakelfard asked.

"I don't know," Isenviole answered. "I stood in her hut myself and saw that she was in a trance!"

"Your eyes must be playing tricks on you!" Hakelfard stated. "You have become weak, and these humans can now fool you!"

"What do you suggest we do now?" Isenviole asked.

"There is nothing more we can do," Hakelfard answered. "I'm still hungry. We missed our feeding session yesterday. We will head west and find another subject. After we feed, we will be able to think more clearly and find these two renegade humans!"

"Perhaps they are dead," Isenviole suggested. "Surely, one of the trees has crushed them and brought them to their deaths."

"And maybe they haven't," Hakelfard replied. "Perhaps they have gotten away. I will not be satisfied until I find their bodies. If we find them soon enough, we can still feast on them! For now, any islander will do."

"I suppose you're right," Isenviole said.

"Aarnshire, can you follow us and keep the crystal active?" Hakelfard asked.

"Of course," Aarnshire replied.

They walked away in search of a new subject to feast on. Soon, they were out of the area. The islander they chose screamed so loudly that her screams almost reached Lakali and Akoni.

Even had they heard, there wouldn't have been anything they could do to help her. The leaders were too far away now, and Lakali and Akoni could have never gotten there in time.

Hours passed, and the sun was starting to set. As darkness began to take over the area, Lakali and Akoni decided it was time to try to emerge from the cave. Akoni went first. If the leaders caught him, he would insist that he had lost Lakali. He would tell them that she must have been killed by the falling trees. He would do anything he could to try to keep them from looking inside the cave.

Akoni climbed out of the cave carefully, having to pull his body up and over a fallen tree that laid on the ground just a couple of feet in front of the cave's entrance.

Looking around to see that the coast appeared to be clear, he whispered to Lakali to join him and helped her out of the cave. They looked around and decided their best bet was to go away from the cave, to go further into the trees and to stay away from the populated areas until they came up with a plan. When they finally felt they had put enough distance between themselves and the fallen trees, they sat down on the ground, leaning back against some coconut palms. Lakali leaned back against Akoni, and Akoni put his arms around her. They were both winded and focused on catching their breath, their hearts racing and their hands shaking. Finally, Akoni whispered and broke the silence.

"I should have believed you sooner," he said. "I'm sorry."

"It's okay," Lakali replied. "The important thing is that you're here with me now."

"You saved my life," Akoni said.

"Nothing that you wouldn't have done for me also," Lakali stated.

"I would give my life to save you," Akoni said truthfully.

"Don't say that," Lakali replied.

"What?" Akoni asked.

"I can't bear the thought of being without you," Lakali answered. "I would rather die than to lose you!"

"Lakali, no!" Akoni scolded her. "Don't ever say that! You must promise me that you will fight to live no matter what happens to me!"

Lakali turned slightly so that she could face Akoni.

"I promise," she said. "But only if you promise to be careful and to do everything you can to not leave me!"

"I promise," Akoni said. "And I promise you something else also. When we get out of this mess, and we *are* going to get out of it, I'm going to put a ring on your finger! I'm going to marry you, and you're going to be my bride."

"Oh, Akoni!" Lakali said as she cried.

Akoni saw the tears slipping down her face.

"Why are you crying?" he asked gently as he wiped the tears from her face.

"Because I love you so much and I fear we will never get out of this mess!" Lakali answered.

"We will. I promise! Please, don't worry. We'll figure something out!" Akoni tried to reassure her.

He drew Lakali closer to him, and she rested her face on his chest.

"Hold me," she said. "And don't ever let go!"

"I won't," Akoni replied. "I'll never let you go."

They slept very restlessly that evening, awaking at the slightest sounds, convinced that the leaders had found them and that their deaths were eminent. When the morning sun lifted its face, the two of them remained still, holding onto each other and trying to formulate a plan.

Lakali pulled herself away from Akoni's chest but sat on the ground with Akoni's arms still wrapped around her.

"What are we going to do?" she asked.

"I'm not sure," Akoni answered. "But I do know one thing. The leaders will be looking for us. We can't stay here."

"Maybe they'll think we were killed by the falling trees," Lakali suggested.

"Something tells me they won't give up until they find us," Akoni worried. "They won't believe we are dead unless they find our bodies. We must keep moving, and we must be on the lookout. We must be careful to not let them find us."

"I can't bear to think of them," Lakali said. "I've never seen anything so hideous! They aren't even human!"

"I know," Akoni said. "It's all like a nightmare."

"And to think they have been feasting on the islanders all this time," Lakali started to cry. "It's so unbearable to think about. Poor Amzi! And now, I know what really happened to my parents also! Oh, Akoni, it's all too much!"

Akoni drew Lakali close to him.

"I'm so sorry," he said. "Tell me again about Amzi. I wish I could remember him. You said he was Caristiona's husband?"

Lakali nodded.

"The two of you were great friends," she said. "When we weren't spending time together, you were usually off doing guy things with him. You were always out hunting for Starfeathers together."

"Did we find any of them?" Akoni asked. "They're my favorite bird, but they are so hard to catch."

"None," Lakali answered. "They always eluded you. It didn't matter, though. You and Amzi would come back laughing like children. You were always telling silly jokes. I loved seeing you so happy."

"It seems a shame I can't remember him," Akoni lamented. "Do you think I'll ever remember him?"

"I don't know," Lakali answered. "Maybe if we could destroy that crystal the leaders are using. Maybe then, everyone's memories would come back."

"You might be right," Akoni replied. "But right now, I'd say we have bigger problems than not being able to remember the past. Like staying alive, for instance, and trying to figure out how to save the other islanders from being eaten!"

"Who do you think they are anyway?" Lakali asked. "Some sort of monsters?"

"We were always taught that monsters don't exist," Akoni said. "But now, well, what else could they be?"

Lakali shrugged.

"I don't know, but I hate them!" she said bitterly. "I hate them for what they're doing to everyone!'

"Me too," Akoni said. "We'll make them pay. I promise!"

Lakali and Akoni looked up at the sky. They could see storm clouds moving in. They knew they needed to find shelter.

"This doesn't look good," Akoni said. "We must find a place to take cover."

They got up and started walking. They could hear the storm coming near them as thunder sounded fiercely in the heavens. They were walking for about ten minutes when they found an old, abandoned cabin secluded in the woods. They walked in and brushed some cobwebs aside.

"What do you suppose this was used for?" Lakali asked.

"I don't know," Akoni answered. "But I'd say that we're lucky to find it."

More thunder sounded. As they looked out the window, they saw a huge streak of lightning come down and hit a tree about fifty yards away from the cabin. Lakali jumped and put her arms around Akoni.

"Hold me," she said, and Akoni held her close.

Fortunately, the storm passed quickly. By now, Lakali and Akoni realized they were getting very hungry. It had been almost eighteen hours since they had last eaten. There was no food in the cabin. It had been abandoned for many years. Akoni walked outside. There were palm trees scattered within the other trees that made up the wooded area. He spotted one with bananas. He took a large fallen stick from the ground to throw and knock some of the fruit loose. He took a couple of bananas to Lakali and grabbed a couple for himself as well. They ate the fruit, grateful to have something to fill their stomachs and to strengthen them. They knew that they needed to keep moving and that they also needed to come up with a plan to defeat their leaders. They knew they were in a crunch for time. Once the clear-thinking session was called, another islander would be killed.

As they started to walk and headed back toward their section, Lakali was already formulating an idea.

"We have to get rid of the crystals," Lakali said. "We have to get them away from the boxes and we have to get as many as possible. The more people who are awake when the clear-thinking session begins, the better!"

"We can't risk taking them to the ocean," Akoni said. "It will be too easy to spot us."

"Maybe we could bury the crystals in the sand," Lakali suggested.

Akoni nodded.

"That might work," he said. "But we have to be careful not to be seen going into the huts. No telling what memories the leaders have already planted in our friends' minds about us."

"You're right," Lakali said. "Section Five isn't safe. As much as I'd like to save my friends, it's too dangerous there. We must start in another section where we aren't so well-known. That way, if we are accidentally spotted, perhaps the people won't know who we are and no one will report us."

"That does sound like the safest plan," Akoni said. "But I'm not sure I could live with myself if I didn't return to our own section and try to save our friends. Do you think you could live with yourself if we neglected them and one of our friends became their next victim?"

Lakali thought about it.

"No," she finally said. "You're right. Just the thought of something happening to Bakita or Caristiona is too much. But I'm afraid. If they tell the leaders we are there…"

"We won't let them see us," Akoni assured her. "We'll take the crystals from our friends first. Then, we'll get as many more as we can. I promise you that I won't let anything happen to you!"

Akoni reached down and kissed Lakali.

"What kind of future husband would I be if I didn't take care of you?" he asked.

Lakali cried again.

"Again with the crying?" Akoni asked. "I thought you would be happy to speak of our marriage."

"Of course I am," Lakali replied. "I'm just afraid we'll never be allowed to marry and will always be hiding from our friends and leaders."

Secretly, that was Akoni's fear also.

"Don't say that," he consoled her. "Everything will work out. Trust me."

Lakali nodded and followed Akoni as they began to make their way back to Section Five, taking care to stay hidden within the trees. When they got there, they were relieved to see that it was one of the busiest times of day. The islanders were hurrying about, doing their chores. No one was near their huts. Lakali and Akoni knew, though, that the leaders would be looking for them, and this was one of the places where they expected them to return.

What Lakali and Akoni didn't know was that two of the leaders were guarding their huts, hidden inside, each taking one hut to stake out, convinced that the two islanders would come back to get their belongings. Fortunately, for Lakali and Akoni, they had no intention of returning to their own huts.

That wasn't their mission. They had more important things to tend to.

They started with Caristiona's hut. Akoni hid behind the hut as Lakali snuck around and opened the door, grateful that no one was around to spot her. She went in and retrieved the crystal, then hurrying to the back of the hut where Akoni stood guard.

They quickly ran from the hut, Lakali trying to resist the urge to return the crystal. It still had a strange power over her. They found a secluded area a few yards away and quickly dug up the sand, burying the crystal as deeply as they dared before moving on. Again at the next hut, the crystal was heavy. It tried to keep Lakali from removing it, but she was stronger now. After seeing the things she had seen, her determination was greater than any power the crystal tried to claim over her.

They continued to two of Akoni's friends' huts and buried their crystals also. Then, they headed to Leilani's hut. Leilani was an older woman who was one of Bakita's close friends. Even though Lakali wasn't as close to Leilani as she was to Bakita, they still enjoyed each other's company.

When Lakali and Akoni got to Leilani's hut, they heard noises inside. It was obvious that Leilani was home. It sounded like she was sweeping the floor of the hut. Lakali wanted to go inside and warn Leilani, but she knew she couldn't. Leilani would never believe her wild story, not even with Akoni backing her up. Surely, they would be turned in. Leilani would think that she was getting them some much-needed help. Sadly, they moved on to the next hut which belonged to Bakita and Hachuo. Akoni hurried inside and retrieved the two crystals. Once outside, Lakali came to his aid and helped bury the crystals as quickly as they could.

Now that they had taken care of as many of their friend's crystals as possible, they methodically went from hut to hut, removing all the crystals that they could, taking care to not be spotted and always keeping an eye out, especially for their leaders.

Several times, they found themselves darting out of view just in time as an unexpected islander came close to spotting them. Fortunately, most of the islanders' work was done away from the housing area, so they didn't have too many close calls.

Altogether, they were able to get rid of thirty-five crystals before they could hear islanders starting to return in too great a number to risk continuing with their task. Akoni and Lakali ducked back into the tree line, staying hidden. They remained there, watching and waiting.

They waited in the trees for about an hour before they saw most of the islanders get a glazed look in their eyes and head in a trance toward their huts. There were many islanders who did not follow them, though. Those were the islanders whose crystals had been buried. They watched the other islanders with confusion, wondering where they were going and why they looked so out of it.

Caristiona was one of the confused islanders. She didn't know why everyone was going into their huts. Was it time for the clear-thinking session? She didn't know. Perhaps she should go into her hut and wait. Surely, it was going to be happening soon. That's why so many people were going into their huts. She headed inside so that she would be ready.

Outside, some of the islanders called to the others, asking them what was going on. But the others ignored them and walked without speaking to their huts, closing the doors behind them. They settled down on their mats and prepared for their clear-thinking sessions.

Lakali and Akoni came out from the trees and hid behind one of the huts, ready to act at a moment's notice. They just hoped that the leaders would choose their section today. They counted on the fact that the leaders would be looking for them, and this was the most logical section where they would be.

Sure enough, they saw two leaders emerge. Lakali pointed and showed Akoni that one of them was coming from her hut. Akoni felt himself tremble, knowing that the leaders had been laying a trap for them and had been there all along as they scrambled from hut to hut.

The leaders looked confused. They didn't know why so many of the islanders were still outside. Why were they not in their huts and why were they awake?

Knowing they had to do something, they started to direct the islanders to their huts, reminding them it was time for their clear-thinking session and commanding them to go look inside their trinket boxes at once. Even though the islanders weren't under the power of the crystals, they trusted their leaders and did as they were commanded. The leaders looked to each other, wondering what to do next.

"Well, we have to assume they are now looking at their crystals," Isenviole said. "Check the doors. Lock them just to be safe."

The huts were equipped to be locked from the outside only. The leaders had instructed the huts to be built in such a manner to make sure they would have a backup plan if needed. While the islanders never understood why they needed outside locks, they had built the huts as they were told, again trusting the wisdom of their leaders.

Akoni and Lakali watched as the leaders went

from hut to hut securing the islanders and making them prisoners. Then, they watched as the leaders approached a hut.

"No!" Lakali couldn't help but say the word aloud, grateful that she was far enough away that the leaders couldn't hear her.

The hut that they were entering belonged to Caristiona. Within moments, Lakali and Akoni heard Caristiona scream.

The other islanders who were still awake heard it too and rushed to their doors, just to find that they were locked inside their huts. They pounded on their doors and demanded to be set free. For a moment, it distracted the leaders. They had hoped that there had been some fluke and that their main crystal had only temporarily malfunctioned, not sending out the signal clearly to everyone to enter their huts and begin their clear-thinking session. But now, they knew something more had gone wrong. Islanders were still awake and weren't under the power of their crystals.

They looked around and scanned the huts while they held onto their intended meal. Caristiona squirmed and tried to free herself. She screamed loudly.

Lakali and Akoni saw that the leaders were searching the area. They hid themselves behind the nearest hut.

"What now?" they could hear Hakelfard ask.

"Ignore them!" Isenviole responded. "We'll deal with them later!"

They continued dragging Caristiona toward the shore. Lakali and Akoni saw their chance. They split up, running from hut to hut, unlocking doors and instructing the islanders to go help Caristiona. Soon, almost three dozen islanders were awake and free, and they all saw Caristiona being dragged down the beach, screaming. The islanders started running and charging toward the leaders and Caristiona.

By now, the leaders heard the commotion behind them. They turned around and saw the angry islanders coming at them. Their bodies immediately metamorphosed into the fish-like beings that they truly were. When the islanders saw the transformation, they were taken aback and were afraid. Some of them stopped running and emitted screams of their own. Others, even though frightened, now knew they must rescue the girl from the monsters who held her in their grip.

Lakali and Akoni rushed to the wood shack and retrieved firewood to fight the leaders with. They had seen how one had been killed easily when the wood had struck him on the head. They ran toward the leaders along with the other islanders. The leaders were running and trying to drag Caristiona with them, but they had been slowed down, distracted by the islanders who were chasing them. Bringing the girl was keeping them from going as fast as they could. The islanders were too close. They would be closing in on them in no time if they didn't pick up their speed.

Regretfully, they released Caristiona. She ran away from the water that had already covered most of her body. The other islanders greeted her. They grabbed the girl and instinctively ran away from the water, away from the monsters.

"No!" Akoni cried. "Don't stop! Go after them!"

But the islanders were frightened. They didn't want to pursue the scary creatures now that they had rescued Caristiona. Akoni and Lakali ran as fast as they could. They were in the water pursuing the leaders. Isenviole got away. Now in fish-like form, he swam swiftly through the water.

But Akoni snagged Hakelfard and flung him backwards, hanging onto his reptilian-like arm. Lakali came and met them. The water came halfway up her thighs. She started to swing the firewood wildly at the leader, being careful to avoid hitting Akoni.

Hakelfard hissed and his fins shot outward to the sides of his face. He emitted a shrill scream, alerting the others.

Isenviole was in the water and heard him, as did Aarnshire who was further down the beach. But Isenviole was frightened. He had seen what had happened to his friend yesterday and didn't want to see his own blood spilled. So, he swam away, anxious to get to Aarnshire and tell him what was happening.

Lakali's aim missed. Hakelfard took his free arm to knock the wood out of her hands, thrusting her backward. As Akoni tried to hold onto Hakelfard with his left hand, he still had the piece of wood in his right hand. In the moment of distraction when Hakelfard flung Lakali away, Akoni swung his firewood and it hit its mark, hitting Hakelfard on the shoulder. He cried out in pain and moved away from Akoni. But in the process, he came closer to Lakali who had retrieved her own club. She swung at him, but she again missed her mark. With his good arm, Hakelfard again flung the club away. Angrily, he lunged at Lakali. He threw his hand around her neck, gripping it tightly and taking her below the water with him.

Akoni panicked. He dove under the water, forgetting his club, his only focus on rescuing Lakali. He saw the two of them struggling underwater, Hakelfard dragging Lakali into deeper water as he held onto her and tried to choke the life out of her. Lakali was trying to get away, but

Hakelfard was holding her too tightly and she couldn't breathe. She could tell she was being dragged slowly out to sea. Akoni came up from behind, wrapping his own arms around Hakelfard's neck, halting him from going any further into the ocean. Using his elbow to tightly grip the leader about the throat, Akoni threatened to cut off Hakelfard's breathing as well. Akoni used his knees and rammed them into Hakelfard's back. The leader's body convulsed, trying to pull away from Akoni. In the process, he lost his grip on Lakali. She was barely conscious, but she was now free.

Even though she could see Akoni and the leader struggling underwater, she needed oxygen! Lakali pushed herself to the surface of the water and breathed rapidly in and out, sucking in the sweet oxygen and trying to catch her breath. Her heart was pounding and felt like it was about to come right out of her chest. She needed to help Akoni, but she was still struggling to breathe, her neck still feeling constricted from the leader's assault.

Under the water, Akoni held Hakelfard tightly. Hakelfard tried to swim away, but Akoni was holding him back. Akoni knew that he couldn't hold him much longer. He was feeling the effect of holding his breath for so long and needed to surface for air. He drew Hakelfard in tighter, not releasing his grip upon his throat.

Finally, he felt the leader start to go limp. He stopped resisting Akoni. Desperate to get air, Akoni released him and Hakelfard's body faced upwards, letting Akoni see his green glowing eyes. As Akoni saw Hakelfard in that fleeting moment, he saw the leader's eyes go dim, the green light dying and his eyes became lifeless. Hakelfard floated below the surface of the water, but he showed no signs of life.

Akoni swam to the surface and gasped for

breath. He spotted Lakali and swam to her.

"Is he dead?" Lakali barely got out the words.

"I think so," Akoni replied. "But I don't think I can go down there to check."

"Then, don't," Lakali said.

Akoni nodded in agreement, and the two of them made their way to shore. Once there, they collapsed on the ground and focused on catching their breath. By now, the other islanders were coming to see if they were okay, still very confused about what had just happened. As they tried to catch their breath, Akoni and Lakali slowly begin to explain to the islanders what had happened.

It was all hard to believe. And yet, they had seen their leaders turn into monsters right in front of their eyes. Caristiona was still shaken up and was trembling from her encounter with the leaders. The islanders had no choice but to believe the crazy story.

The rest of the islanders were still under the power of the crystal. The ones who were awake knew what they had to do. They began going from hut to hut, being careful to avert their eyes from the crystals and close the boxes, awaking the islanders from their trances. Slowly, the islanders began to emerge from their huts. No one seemed to believe the crazy story they were being told, yet the ones who had been awake insisted that they were telling the truth. Those who had just come out of their clear-thinking sessions didn't know what to believe.

By now, Isenviole had made his way to Aarnshire. He told Aarnshire what had happened and that they could assume that Hakelfard was dead. It was now just the two of them. Aarnshire was furious. In such a short time, their numbers had been cut in half! It was hard to believe that they were the only two left now.

Angrily, Aarnshire lifted the purple crystal, willing it to rain down a terrible storm upon the island. The islanders on the beach scattered and tried to find safety. It was a storm so severe, such as they had never seen before. They had to run far from the beach as giant waves came from the ocean, snatching a few of them and pulling them into the ocean. Lightning strikes came in rapid succession. No place seemed safe as the strikes hit the ground again and again and again.

Islanders were screaming and scattering everywhere. It was every man and woman for themselves. Lakali and Akoni stuck together, and Caristiona stayed close to them. The three of them ran away from the beach and ran into the tree line, not stopping to look behind them. They had to dodge out of the way many times as trees were struck down and nearly crashed down upon them. The wind picked up speed and was so strong that at one point, it lifted Caristiona and flung her about twenty feet ahead of their path. When she crashed down on the ground, her ankle was injured severely and she couldn't walk. Akoni picked her up and carried her as he and Lakali kept plunging ahead.

Finally, Aarnshire was exhausted. He couldn't keep the crystal going anymore. It took too much concentration to create such a storm. He released the crystal, and a tear slipped down his face as he thought of his fallen friends.

"What are we going to do now?" Isenviole asked.

"I don't know," Aarnshire replied. "We are so outnumbered now. I fear we aren't strong enough to deal with these islanders by ourselves. As much as I would love to kill them all and take vengeance for what they have done, I fear if we stay and fight them, our own lives will be lost as well."

"So, you are suggesting we leave?" Isenviole asked.

"What choice do we have?" Aarnshire answered.

"But we have been here so long," Isenviole replied. "This is the only home we have ever known on this planet."

Aarnshire let out a hiss, not out of anger but out of sadness as he remembered his home planet that they had had to evacuate in such a hurry so long ago as the giant meteor had raced to destroy it. They had barely gotten their ship out in time before seeing their planet destroyed. The other ships had tried to make it out as well, but they hadn't been fast enough. The four of them were the only ones to make it out alive. No females had escaped with them. They knew that they were the last four Baltinithonians to still exist. They would never be able to repopulate their species. And now, their numbers were down to two.

Baltinithonians had a long lifespan. Even though they were hundreds of years old, they were barely reaching their middle-aged years. It seemed a shame that they were now in this predicament. Yes, they had shared a very sad past, but they had grown accustomed to the island. The inhabitants made a good food source, their flesh tasty and their minds so easily manipulated.

"It's a large planet," Aarnshire said. "I'm sure there are other vulnerable humans somewhere and another nearby island that we can find and take up residence."

"We haven't used the ship in so long," Isenviole said. "Do you suppose it's still functional?"

"I don't see why it shouldn't be," Aarnshire replied. "Our ships were made to survive extreme elements and to last for centuries when they were crafted back on Baltinithonia."

Isenviole nodded.

"I suppose you're right," Isenviole said. "It is regretful, though. I truly thought I would live out my life here."

"As did I," Aarnshire agreed. "But there's nothing more we can do about it."

"Should we retrieve the crystals before we leave?" Isenviole asked.

"It's too dangerous," Aarnshire answered. "No telling how many islanders they have on their side now. Thankfully, there are still a few hundred crystals tucked away on the ship, more than enough to get more humans under our control. We will just have to be careful to find another uninhabited island and only pull in a small number of islanders at a time. No more worrying about keeping a five-year supply. Perhaps that was our downfall. We had too many humans under our control at once. It will be better to keep a couple hundred or so and feed off of them, pulling more in when necessary."

His friend nodded in agreement.

"Well then, I suppose we should go before more trouble comes our way," Isenviole said.

Aarnshire took one more look at the island he had called home for so long. He would also miss this place, but he knew that he and his friend had to secure their future. He turned and, carrying the crystal, he hurried with Isenviole to the water. Once in the water, they swam rapidly out toward the ship which sat on the floor of the ocean hundreds of yards out. Once there, they entered the ship and set the controls, ready to leave and take off in search of a new home.

As the leaders prepared to leave, another great storm came upon the whole island. Lightning filled the sky and darted from cloud to cloud. Rain pummeled the ground and water, and some of the lightning strikes made their way to the ground although most of it stayed within the sky.

    Giving out an exasperated sigh at the thought of leaving the only place he had known as home for so long, Aarnshire put the ship into gear as a tear slipped down his face. Slowly, the great ship started to move. It picked up speed quickly as it sailed under the water and took them far away from the island that they had known as home for so long.

Chapter 13

As the ship left the island, Lakali and Akoni heard a shrill hum and looked out to the ocean. After the first storm had cleared, they had come back out to shore. They were looking to retreat from the new storm when they heard the hum and couldn't help but stop and watch. What they saw amazed them! The waves in the ocean reversed. Instead of coming to shore, they followed the ship out to sea like a giant riptide. The ship emitted a glowing green light so bright that the remnants of the light skirted the ocean's surface.

Once the ship was out of sight, the skies cleared and the lightning stopped. The sun came out, and the day was bright. The waves came back and rolled gently onto the shoreline.

"What does this all mean?" Lakali asked. "Did you see that? It was incredible!"

"I did," Akoni replied. "And I think it means we have hope. I believe what we just saw was the rest of our leaders leaving the island!"

Lakali looked out to the ocean. Could Akoni be right? Could they be free of their leaders once and for all? She began to shake softly as the tears slipped down her cheeks. Akoni drew her close.

"Lakali, what is it?" he asked. "Everything is okay now."

"Oh, Akoni, I do hope so!" Lakali said, looking up at the man she loved with all of her heart.

She returned her gaze to the ocean, almost half-expecting to see the glowing green light come back and to be plagued by their leaders again. But the ocean was calm. The waves were coming in toward the shore as normal. Out in the distance, Lakali even caught a glimpse of a couple of dolphins jumping in the waves and playing.

"I wonder," Lakali mused. "Where will they go? What will they do?"

"I don't know," Akoni said. "But we can't let ourselves worry about them now. I pity whoever they come across."

Lakali nodded and leaned her head onto Akoni's chest.

As they stood on the beach close enough to the water for it to spill over their feet, they looked to the island. Complete chaos was forming. Everyone was confused and frightened. Akoni and Lakali began to hear a familiar voice.

"Amzi! Amzi! Where are you?!" Caristiona desperately searched for the husband she would never see again.

"Amzi!" Akoni suddenly nearly shouted. "I remember Amzi!"

Lakali wasn't sure how to feel about his newfound memory. She had a suspicion that the islanders' memories were coming back now that the purple crystal had disappeared with the ship. But did she want people to remember? Would it be too painful? She watched her dear friend searching desperately for Amzi. How could she ever explain to Caristiona what had happened? Perhaps her friend would be better off just thinking that her husband had disappeared. Lakali began to have visions of her parents, but she tried to push them aside, the thought of now knowing what had truly happened to them being too fresh and painful to allow herself to remember them yet.

"You remember Amzi?" Lakali asked.

"Yes," Akoni said sadly. "He was a good friend. He didn't deserve what happened to him."

Now, Akoni let a tear slip down his face.

Other voices drifted among the frightened conversations. A young man, who was on his honeymoon aboard a private yacht with his new bride when the beauty of the island beckoned him to come and stay here, was searching desperately for his wife. He hurried through the crowd calling her name over and over, but he couldn't find Becky anywhere.

"I doubt this Becky is anywhere to be found," Akoni said. "She was probably one of their victims also."

Lakali drew herself close to Akoni. How close she had come to losing him. She shuddered at the very thought of what had happened when the leaders had tried to drag him out to sea.

Another voice sounded above the others.

"Mr. President! Mr. President! Oh, thank goodness! There you are!"

The voice came from a person that Lakali and Akoni didn't know well. He was a quiet man named Bashikiro who had kept to himself most of the time. In a previous life, he had held an important position with the Secret Service. He would have guarded this man he called "Mr. President" with his life. But what shocked Lakali and Akoni was when they saw who Bashikiro was talking to. It was Hachuo! Hachuo looked as confused as Lakali and Akoni did. President. That was a strange word. Lakali and Akoni had never heard it before.

"Where am I?" Hachuo was asking Bashikiro.

"I don't know," Bashikiro replied. "I know we've been here a long time, but I don't know why."

"I remember the plane going down," Hachuo replied. "The pilot was calling for help. I never expected Air Force One to go down like that. It wasn't like we were attacked. Or were we? Couldn't anyone find us? Why haven't they come to get us off this island?"

"I don't know," Bashikiro replied.

Bakita came running up and threw her arms around her husband.

"Hachuo!" she cried. "You're alright! I've been looking all over for you!"

Hachuo was confused. His wife spoke the name he had become accustomed to for so many years, twenty years in fact since his plane had gone down. But he didn't know why this was his name now. He remembered the name he had so long ago, back when he had barely been president for a year before coming to the island.

Wife? Yes, Bakita was his wife. But what about Lisa? He thought about the woman who had proudly served beside him as First Lady. Where was she? That's right. She was back home. She surely assumed him to be dead by now. But why did he have another wife? It didn't make sense. Lisa was the love of his life. He would never cheat on her.

So, the stories continued among the islanders. About a third of them had been recent arrivals, coming to the island sometime within the last couple of decades, having new memories implanted in them as soon as they came and having past memories erased. Now that they were no longer under the power of the crystals, their memories came back and mass confusion was setting in among many of the islanders.

For the other islanders who had been born on the island and had spent their whole lives here, they weren't plagued with trying to figure out what they were doing on the island. Instead, images of people who had been friends and family members rushed through their heads. Where were these people? What had happened to them?

As they looked around, it also suddenly struck many of the islanders how odd it was that there were so few older people. The leaders had left some middle-aged people on the island, giving the islanders hope of reaching old age. However, there was no one over fifty left alive. If they let them live too long, their flesh would become too old and tough. None of the leaders had wanted that.

People who had come to the island, whether by plane or ship, tried to find those they had travelled with. They looked desperately for a way off of the island. When they saw the fishing boats, they began to plan a way to go and get help for all of the people who were stranded on the island.

While Akoni and Lakali still felt a little afraid, worried that the leaders might come back, they had no desire to leave the island. This was the only place they had ever called home. They wouldn't know what to do anywhere else. They stood on the beach with their arms wrapped around each other, watching the chaos around them.

"Do you think they'll be alright?" Lakali asked.

"Who?" Akoni inquired.

"All of them," Lakali answered. "Just look at them. They seem so lost."

Akoni *had* been watching. Had it not been so grim, it might have been a little funny watching how crazy they all looked as they scattered everywhere, trying to get a grip on what had happened.

"They'll be fine," he said. "I'm sure of it. Now that the leaders are gone, we'll all be fine. It'll take time, but life is going to be good again. Just wait and see."

"Oh, I do hope so," Lakali said. "Do you think the crystals in the trinket boxes still pose a danger? Should we get rid of them?"

"I think they're harmless now that the leaders are gone," Akoni replied. "But just from the bad memories alone, I don't want to ever see mine again!"

"Me either," Lakali agreed. "Do you think the leaders will ever return?"

"I doubt it," Akoni said. "They know they are outnumbered and have been found out. They'll be too scared to risk it."

About that time, Lakali heard a familiar meow.

"It looks like someone else is confused also," Akoni said.

"Yeah, I guess Nightfall isn't too crazy about all the commotion. But at least, he's safe now, just like the rest of us," Lakali replied.

"I'm sure you'll have him consoled in no time at all. That cat loves you," Akoni said.

Lakali smiled. Yes, she knew the cat was fond of her. She was fond of him also. But right now, as much as she liked Nightfall, there were other concerns on her mind.

"What should we tell Caristiona and the others?" Lakali asked.

Akoni thought about it for a moment.

"I think if we tell them the whole story, most people won't believe us and will just think we're crazy," he finally answered. "Even worse, if they *do* believe us, the truth of what happened to their loved ones who have gone missing will be too much. I think we should pretend to be as confused as everyone else. In time, all of the craziness will die down."

"But what about the ones we already told?" Lakali asked.

"We'll say we can't remember anything," Akoni answered. "They'll believe us and think that the crystals took our memories."

"I think you're right," Lakali said. "I do pity Caristiona, though. I kind of wish she couldn't remember Amzi now that there's nothing we can do to bring him back."

Akoni thought about it.

"If it were me, I would want to remember you," he said. "Even with the pain of losing you, I would never want to be without the memory of what we had together."

He leaned down and kissed Lakali on her forehead. He didn't know why, but a peaceful feeling came over him.

"Thank you for saving my life," he said.

"There's no life I would rather save," Lakali replied.

"So," Akoni said and pulled away from Lakali.

He got down on one knee and looked up at her. Lakali looked down at him and knew what he was doing. Despite the madness around them, a smile spread slowly across her face.

"What are you doing?" she inquired.

"What do you think I'm doing?" Akoni asked.

Lakali smiled down at him.

"Go on," she encouraged him.

"I don't have a ring on me, but I still have to ask," he said. "Will you do me the honor of marrying me?"

"Oh, Akoni! Of course I will!" Lakali said.

Akoni stood up and drew Lakali close. He leaned down and kissed his bride-to-be. Lakali blocked out all of the noise around her and kissed Akoni back, never happier than she was at that moment. Whatever horror had happened to them and no matter how hard the next few months would be as the islanders tried to put their lives together again, Lakali knew that she and Akoni were going to be alright. She knew that they could face anything as long as they faced it together. Finally, Akoni was going to put a ring on her finger!

Author's Notes

I would like to give a special thank you to my sister, Elsie Cochren, who has always been there for me and continues to support me in my writing career.

If you enjoyed this book, please consider leaving an online review or rating it. Reviews and ratings help authors gain much-needed exposure and are appreciated.

To review this book on Amazon, please go to: https://www.amazon.com/Islanders-Sallie-Cochren-ebook/dp/B07RXVRZZL/ref=sr_1_1?dchild=1&keywords=sallie+cochren+islanders&qid=1631989809&sr=8-1

Review this book on Goodreads: https://www.goodreads.com/book/show/42960582-the-islanders

Video trailers and more are available on the author's website at http://www.salliecochren.com

Follow Sallie on Twitter: https://twitter.com/sallie_cochren

Follow Sallie on Facebook:

https://www.facebook.com/pages/category/Author/Sallie-Cochren-1235247979868999/

Follow Sallie on Instagram:
https://www.instagram.com/aliencatsauthor/

Other Books by the Author

"The Voinico's Daughter: A Vânător Vampire Hunter Novel" *(Horror, Vampires)* When Nicoleta goes to Romania and discovers that by birthright, she is meant to be a vampire hunter, will she be able to keep herself and her friends safe? Two of the most powerful vampires, Varujan and Antanasia, have been waiting for her, knowing that Nicoleta will eventually make her way to Romania and face her destiny. Unlike the other vampire hunters, Nicoleta hasn't been training her whole life to kill vampires. In fact, she hasn't trained for it at all. Can she ever become strong enough to take on Antanasia and Varujan in the battle that's inevitably coming?

"The Hungry Sea" *(Dark Fantasy)* Katrina has always loved being near the water. But when a distant voice calls to her from out on the horizon, will she ever be able to figure out its sinister plans? Will she be able to fight the urge to "come and play" as the voice beckons her to do, or will the sea finally claim her for its own?

"No Time to Panic" *(Short Story collection)*
    "The Keepers of the Lights" – *(Horror)* Monsters in the woods want to get free to terrorize the village.
    "The Sheriff's Son" – *(Science Fiction)* People are dying in a small town, only they aren't acting like they're dead!

"The Lightning Tunnel" – *(Science Fiction)* The latest attraction at Thundering Sands Amusement Park isn't what it seems to be. When Mason is transported back in time, will he ever find his way home?

"Traffic Stop" – *(Psychological Thriller)* When Angela and her neighbor are pulled over on what is supposed to be a routine traffic stop, everything quickly changes. Angela is thrown into a nightmare, and it will take everything she has to be able to figure out how to stay alive when she becomes Roger's prisoner. Can she escape in time, or will she become another victim of a psychotic killer?

"The Storm Keepers" – *(Science Fiction)* When strangers arrive with an uncanny ability to predict the weather, can the villagers trust them or do they have a dark agenda?

"The Friend" *(Horror)* Meet Aisha, Jessica's imaginary friend. Does Aisha really have Jessica's best interest at heart? When Aisha's evil nature leads her to kill, everyone may be in danger.

"Alien Cats" Series – *(Humorous Science Fiction Fantasy)* On Katonia, the Persians and Siamese cats work together to rule the distant planet. But the evil-hearted DurPlunk has plans of his own to become the planet's ruler. In book 1, **"No Place Like Home,"** DurPlunk plots with his Sphynx soldiers to find a way to overthrow the Royals. In book 2, ***"Return to Katonia,"*** DurPlunk kidnaps the planet's ruler, Sunset. In book 3, ***"DurPlunk's***

Battle for Planet Earth," DurPlunk has a new planet to try to conquer. Earth! Follow the good-hearted felines and their allies in this fun science fiction adventure!

"The Missing People of Her Dreams" (*Christian Fantasy*) Michelle's premonitions aren't typical. Every vision she has includes a hero who saves the day. But when the tragedies play out for real, those heroes aren't there and people die. Michelle has spent her whole life denying God's existence. But as the visions continue, is God trying to reveal something important to her? Can Michelle ever figure out who the missing people in her dreams are?

Made in the USA
Columbia, SC
12 December 2021